IN THE SPRING

Maupassant Original Short Stories

Volume V

Guy de Maupassant

iBoo Press
London

IN THE SPRING

Maupassant Original Short Stories

Volume V

Guy de Maupassant

Translated by
ALBERT M. C. McMASTER, B.A.
A. E. HENDERSON, B.A.
MME: QUESADA and Others

Layout & Cover © Copyright 2020 iBooPress, London

Published by
iBoo Press House

3rd Floor
86-90 Paul Street
London, EC2A4NE UK

t: +44 20 3695 0809
info@iboo.com II iBoo.com

ISBN
978-1-64181-743-1 (p)

We care about the environment. This paper used in this publication is both acid free and totally chlorine-free (TCF). It meets the minumum requirements of ANSI / NISO z39-49-1992 (r 1997)

Printed in the United States

IN THE SPRING

Maupassant Original Short Stories

Volume V

Guy de Maupassant

VOLUME V

MONSIEUR PARENT	7
QUEEN HORTENSE	31
TIMBUCTOO	38
TOMBSTONES	44
MADEMOISELLE PEARL	51
THE THIEF	64
CLAIR DE LUNE	68
WAITER, A "BOCK"	73
AFTER	79
FORGIVENESS	84
IN THE SPRING	89
A QUEER NIGHT IN PARIS	95

MONSIEUR PARENT

George's father was sitting in an iron chair, watching his little son with concentrated affection and attention, as little George piled up the sand into heaps during one of their walks. He would take up the sand with both hands, make a mound of it, and put a chestnut leaf on top. His father saw no one but him in that public park full of people.

The sun was just disappearing behind the roofs of the Rue Saint-Lazare, but still shed its rays obliquely on that little, overdressed crowd. The chestnut trees were lighted up by its yellow rays, and the three fountains before the lofty porch of the church had the appearance of liquid silver.

Monsieur Parent, accidentally looking up at the church clock, saw that he was five minutes late. He got up, took the child by the arm, shook his dress, which was covered with sand, wiped his hands, and led him in the direction of the Rue Blanche. He walked quickly, so as not to get in after his wife, and the child could not keep up with him. He took him up and carried him, though it made him pant when he had to walk up the steep street. He was a man of forty, already turning gray, and rather stout. At last he reached his house. An old servant who had brought him up, one of those trusted servants who are the tyrants of families, opened the door to him.

"Has madame come in yet?" he asked anxiously.

The servant shrugged her shoulders:

"When have you ever known madame to come home at half-past six, monsieur?"

"Very well; all the better; it will give me time to change my things, for I am very warm."

The servant looked at him with angry and contemptuous pity. "Oh, I can see that well enough," she grumbled. "You are covered with perspiration, monsieur. I suppose you walked quickly and carried the child, and only to have to wait until half-past seven, perhaps, for madame. I have made up my mind not to have dinner ready on time. I shall get it for eight o'clock, and if, you have to wait, I cannot help it; roast meat ought not to be burnt!"

Monsieur Parent pretended not to hear, but went into his own room, and as soon as he got in, locked the door, so as to be alone, quite alone. He was so used now to being abused and badly treated that he never thought himself safe except when he was locked in.

What could he do? To get rid of Julie seemed to him such a formidable thing to do that he hardly ventured to think of it, but it was just as impossible to uphold her against his wife, and before another month the situation would become unbearable between the two. He remained sitting there, with his arms hanging down, vaguely trying to discover some means to set matters straight, but without success. He said to himself: "It is lucky that I have George; without him I should be very miserable."

Just then the clock struck seven, and he started up. Seven o'clock, and he had not even changed his clothes. Nervous and breathless, he undressed, put on a clean shirt, hastily finished his toilet, as if he had been expected in the next room for some event of extreme importance, and went into the drawing-room, happy at having nothing to fear. He glanced at the newspaper, went and looked out of the window, and then sat down again, when the door opened, and the boy came in, washed, brushed, and smiling. Parent took him up in his arms and kissed him passionately; then he tossed him into the air, and held him up to the ceiling, but soon sat down again, as he was tired with all his exertion. Then, taking George on his knee, he made him ride a-cock-horse. The child laughed and clapped his hands and shouted with pleasure, as did his father, who laughed until his big stomach shook, for it amused him almost more than it did the child.

Parent loved him with all the heart of a weak, resigned, ill-used man. He loved him with mad bursts of affection, with caresses and with all the bashful tenderness which was hidden in him, and which had never found an outlet, even at the early period of his married life, for his wife had always shown herself cold and reserved.

Just then Julie came to the door, with a pale face and glistening eyes, and said in a voice which trembled with exasperation: "It is half-past seven, monsieur."

Parent gave an uneasy and resigned look at the clock and replied: "Yes, it certainly is half-past seven."

"Well, my dinner is quite ready now."

Seeing the storm which was coming, he tried to turn it aside. "But did you not tell me when I came in that it would not be ready before eight?"

"Eight! what are you thinking about? You surely do not mean to let the child dine at eight o'clock? It would ruin his stomach. Just suppose that he only had his mother to look after him! She cares a great deal about her child. Oh, yes, we will speak about her; she is a mother! What a pity it is that there should be any mothers like her!"

Parent thought it was time to cut short a threatened scene. "Julie," he said, "I will not allow you to speak like that of your mistress. You understand me, do you not? Do not forget it in the future."

The old servant, who was nearly choked with surprise, turned and went out, slamming the door so violently after her that the lustres on the chandelier rattled, and for some seconds it sounded as if a number of little invisible bells were ringing in the drawing-room.

Eight o'clock struck, the door opened, and Julie came in again. She had lost her look of exasperation, but now she put on an air of cold and determined resolution, which was still more formidable.

"Monsieur," she said, "I served your mother until the day of her death, and I have attended to you from your birth until now, and I think it may be said that I am devoted to the family." She waited for a reply, and Parent stammered:

"Why, yes, certainly, my good Julie."

"You know quite well," she continued, "that I have never done anything for the sake of money, but always for your sake; that I have never deceived you nor lied to you, that you have never had to find fault with me—"

"Certainly, my good Julie."

"Very well, then, monsieur; it cannot go on any longer like this. I have said nothing, and left you in your ignorance, out of respect and liking for you, but it is too much, and every one in the neighborhood is laughing at you. Everybody knows about it, and so I must tell you also, although I do not like to repeat it. The reason why madame comes in at any time she chooses is that she is doing abominable things."

He seemed stupefied and not to understand, and could only stammer out:

"Hold your tongue; you know I have forbidden you——"

But she interrupted him with irresistible resolution. "No, monsieur, I must tell you everything now. For a long time madame has been carrying on with Monsieur Limousin. I have seen them kiss scores of times behind the door. Ah! you may be sure that if Monsieur Limousin had been rich, madame would never have married Monsieur Parent. If you remember how the marriage was brought about, you would understand the matter from beginning to end."

Parent had risen, and stammered out, his face livid: "Hold your tongue —hold your tongue, or——"

She went on, however: "No, I mean to tell you everything. She married you from interest, and she deceived you from the very first day. It was all settled between them beforehand. You need only reflect for a few moments to understand it, and then, as she was not satisfied with having married you, as she did not love you, she has made your life miserable, so miserable that it has almost broken my heart when I have seen it."

He walked up and down the room with hands clenched, repeating: "Hold your tongue—hold your tongue——" For he could find nothing else to say. The old servant, however, would not yield; she seemed resolved on everything.

George, who had been at first astonished and then frightened at those angry voices, began to utter shrill screams, and remained behind his father, with his face puckered up and his mouth open, roaring.

His son's screams exasperated Parent, and filled him with rage and courage. He rushed at Julie with both arms raised, ready to strike her, exclaiming: "Ah! you wretch. You will drive the child out of his senses." He already had his hand on her, when she screamed in his face:

"Monsieur, you may beat me if you like, me who reared you, but that will not prevent your wife from deceiving you, or alter the fact that your child is not yours——"

He stopped suddenly, let his arms fall, and remained standing opposite to her, so overwhelmed that he could understand nothing more.

"You need only to look at the child," she added, "to know who is its father! He is the very image of Monsieur Limousin. You need only look at his eyes and forehead. Why, a blind man could not be mistaken in him."

He had taken her by the shoulders, and was now shaking her with all his might. "Viper, viper!" he said. "Go out the room, viper! Go out, or I shall kill you! Go out! Go out!"

And with a desperate effort he threw her into the next room. She fell across the table, which was laid for dinner, breaking the glasses. Then, rising to her feet, she put the table between her master and herself. While he was pursuing her, in order to take hold of her again, she flung terrible words at him.

Guy de Maupassant

"You need only go out this evening after dinner, and come in again immediately, and you will see! You will see whether I have been lying! Just try it, and you will see." She had reached the kitchen door and escaped, but he ran after her, up the back stairs to her bedroom, into which she had locked herself, and knocking at the door, he said:

"You will leave my house this very instant!"

"You may be certain of that, monsieur," was her reply. "In an hour's time I shall not be here any longer."

He then went slowly downstairs again, holding on to the banister so as not to fall, and went back to the drawing-room, where little George was sitting on the floor, crying. He fell into a chair, and looked at the child with dull eyes. He understood nothing, knew nothing more; he felt dazed, stupefied, mad, as if he had just fallen on his head, and he scarcely even remembered the dreadful things the servant had told him. Then, by degrees, his mind, like muddy water, became calmer and clearer, and the abominable revelations began to work in his heart.

He was no longer thinking of George. The child was quiet now and sitting on the carpet; but, seeing that no notice was being taken of him, he began to cry. His father ran to him, took him in his arms, and covered him with kisses. His child remained to him, at any rate! What did the rest matter? He held him in his arms and pressed his lips to his light hair, and, relieved and composed, he whispered:

"George—my little George—my dear little George——" But he suddenly remembered what Julie had said! Yes, she had said that he was Limousin's child. Oh! it could not be possible, surely. He could not believe it, could not doubt, even for a moment, that he was his own child. It was one of those low scandals which spring from servants' brains! And he repeated: "George—my dear little George." The youngster was quiet again, now that his father was fondling him.

Parent felt the warmth of the little chest penetrate through his clothes, and it filled him with love, courage, and happiness; that gentle warmth soothed him, fortified him and saved him. Then he put the small, curly head away from him a little, and looked at it affectionately, still repeating: "George! Oh, my little George!" But suddenly he thought:

"Suppose he were to resemble Limousin, after all!" He looked at him with haggard, troubled eyes, and tried to discover whether there was any likeness in his forehead, in his nose, mouth, or cheeks. His thoughts wandered as they do when a person is going mad, and his child's face changed in his eyes, and assumed a strange look and improbable resemblances.

The hall bell rang. Parent gave a bound as if a bullet had gone through him. "There she is," he said. "What shall I do?" And he ran and locked himself up in his room, to have time to bathe his eyes. But in a few moments another ring at the bell made him jump again, and then he remembered that Julie had left, without the housemaid knowing it, and so nobody would go to open the door. What was he to do? He went himself, and suddenly he felt brave, resolute, ready for dissimulation and the struggle. The terrible blow had matured him in a few moments. He wished to know the truth, he desired it with the rage of a timid man, and with the tenacity of an easy-going man who has been exasperated.

Nevertheless, he trembled. Does one know how much excited cowardice there often is in boldness? He went to the door with furtive steps, and stopped to listen; his heart beat furiously. Suddenly, however, the noise of the bell over his head startled him like an explosion. He seized the lock, turned the key, and opening the door, saw his wife and Limousin standing before him on the stairs.

With an air of astonishment, which also betrayed a little irritation, she said:

"So you open the door now? Where is Julie?"

His throat felt tight and his breathing was labored as he tried to reply, without being able to utter a word.

"Are you dumb?" she continued. "I asked you where Julie is?"

"She—she—has—gone——" he managed to stammer.

His wife began to get angry. "What do you mean by gone? Where has she gone? Why?"

By degrees he regained his coolness. He felt an intense hatred rise up in him for that insolent woman who was standing before him.

"Yes, she has gone altogether. I sent her away."

"You have sent away Julie? Why, you must be mad."

"Yes, I sent her away because she was insolent, and because—because she was ill-using the child."

"Julie?"

"Yes—Julie."

"What was she insolent about?"

"About you."

"About me?"

"Yes, because the dinner was burnt, and you did not come in."

"And she said——"

"She said—offensive things about you—which I ought not—which I could not listen to——"

"What did she, say?"

"It is no good repeating them."

"I want to hear them."

"She said it was unfortunate for a man like me to be married to a woman like you, unpunctual, careless, disorderly, a bad mother, and a bad wife."

The young woman had gone into the anteroom, followed by Limousin, who did not say a word at this unexpected condition of things. She shut the door quickly, threw her cloak on a chair, and going straight up to her husband, she stammered out:

"You say? You say? That I am——"

Very pale and calm, he replied: "I say nothing, my dear. I am simply repeating what Julie said to me, as you wanted to know what it was, and I wish you to remark that I turned her off just on account of what she said."

She trembled with a violent longing to tear out his beard and scratch his face. In his voice and manner she felt that he was asserting his position as master. Although she had nothing to say by way of reply, she tried to assume the offensive by saying something unpleasant. "I suppose you have had dinner?" she asked.

"No, I waited for you."

She shrugged her shoulders impatiently. "It is very stupid of you to wait after half-past seven," she said. "You might have guessed that I was detained, that I had a good many things to do, visits and shopping,"

And then, suddenly, she felt that she wanted to explain how she had spent her time, and told him in abrupt, haughty words that, having to buy some furniture in a shop a long distance off, very far off, in the Rue de Rennes, she had met Limousin at past seven o'clock on the Boulevard Saint-Germain, and that then she had gone with him to have something to eat in a restaurant, as she did not like to go to one by herself, although she was faint with hunger. That was how she had dined with Limousin, if it could be called dining, for they had only some soup and half a chicken, as they were in a great hurry to get back.

Parent replied simply: "Well, you were quite right. I am not finding fault with you."

Then Limousin, who, had not spoken till then, and who had been half hidden behind Henriette, came forward and put out his hand, saying: "Are you very well?"

Parent took his hand, and shaking it gently, replied: "Yes, I am very well."

But the young woman had felt a reproach in her husband's last words. "Finding fault! Why do you speak of finding fault? One might think that you meant to imply something."

"Not at all," he replied, by way of excuse. "I simply meant that I was not at all anxious although you were late, and that I did not find fault with you for it."

She, however, took the high hand, and tried to find a pretext for a quarrel. "Although I was late? One might really think that it was one o'clock in the morning, and that I spent my nights away from home."

"Certainly not, my dear. I said late because I could find no other word. You said you should be back at half-past six, and you returned at half-past eight. That was surely being late. I understand it perfectly well. I am not at all surprised, even. But—but—I can hardly use any other word."

"But you pronounce them as if I had been out all night."

"Oh, no-oh, no!"

She saw that he would yield on every point, and she was going into her own room, when at last she noticed that George was screaming, and then she asked, with some feeling: "What is the matter with the child?"

"I told you that Julie had been rather unkind to him."

"What has the wretch been doing to him?"

"Oh nothing much. She gave him a push, and he fell down."

She wanted to see her child, and ran into the dining room, but stopped short at the sight of the table covered with spilt wine, with broken decanters and glasses and overturned saltcellars. "Who did all that mischief?" she asked.

"It was Julie, who——" But she interrupted him furiously:

"That is too much, really! Julie speaks of me as if I were a shameless woman, beats my child, breaks my plates and dishes, turns my house upside down, and it appears that you think it all quite natural."

"Certainly not, as I have got rid of her."

"Really! You have got rid of her! But you ought to have given her in charge. In such cases, one ought to call in the Commissary of Police!"

"But—my dear—I really could not. There was no reason. It would have been very difficult——"

She shrugged her shoulders disdainfully. "There! you will never be anything but a poor, wretched fellow, a man without a will, without any firmness or energy. Ah! she must have said some nice things to you, your Julie, to make you turn her off like that. I should like to have been here for a minute, only for a minute." Then she opened the drawing-room door and ran to George, took him into her arms and kissed him, and said: "Georgie, what is it, my darling, my pretty one, my treasure?"

Then, suddenly turning to another idea, she said: "But the child has had no dinner? You have had nothing to eat, my pet?"

"No, mamma."

Then she again turned furiously upon her husband. "Why, you must be mad, utterly mad! It is half-past eight, and George has had no dinner!"

He excused himself as best he could, for he had nearly lost his wits through the overwhelming scene and the explanation, and felt crushed by this ruin of his life. "But, my dear, we were waiting for you, as I did not wish to dine without you. As you come home late every day, I expected you every moment."

She threw her bonnet, which she had kept on till then, into an easy-chair, and in an angry voice she said: "It is really intolerable to have to do with people who can understand nothing, who can divine nothing and do nothing by themselves. So, I suppose, if I were to come in at twelve o'clock at night, the child would have had nothing to eat? Just as if you could not have understood that, as it was after half-past seven, I was prevented from coming home, that I had met with some hindrance!"

Parent trembled, for he felt that his anger was getting the upper hand, but Limousin interposed, and turning toward the young woman, said:

"My dear friend, you, are altogether unjust. Parent could not guess that you would come here so late, as you never do so, and then, how could you expect him to get over the difficulty all by himself, after having sent away Julie?"

But Henriette was very angry, and replied:

"Well, at any rate, he must get over the difficulty himself, for I will not help him," she replied. "Let him settle it!" And she went into her own room, quite forgetting that her child had not had anything to eat.

Limousin immediately set to work to help his friend. He picked up the broken glasses which strewed the table and took them out, replaced the plates and knives and forks, and put the child into his high chair, while Parent went to look for the chambermaid to wait at table. The girl came in, in great astonishment, as she had heard nothing in George's room, where she had been working.

She soon, however, brought in the soup, a burnt leg of mutton, and mashed potatoes.

Parent sat by the side of the child, very much upset and distressed at all that had happened. He gave the boy his dinner, and endeavored to eat something himself, but he could only swallow with an effort, as his throat felt paralyzed. By degrees he was seized with an insane desire to look at Limousin, who was sitting opposite to him, making bread pellets, to see whether George was like him, but he did not venture to raise his eyes for some time. At last, however, he made up his mind to do so, and gave a quick, sharp look at the face which he knew so well, although he almost fancied that he had never examined it carefully. It looked so different to what he had imagined. From time to time he looked at Limousin, trying to recognize a likeness in the smallest lines of his face, in the slightest features, and then he looked at his son, under the pretext of feeding him.

Two words were sounding in his ears: "His father! his father! his father!" They buzzed in his temples at every beat of his heart. Yes, that man, that tranquil man who was sitting on the other side of the table, was, perhaps, the father of his son, of George, of his little George. Parent left off eating; he could not swallow any more. A terrible pain, one of those attacks of pain which make men scream, roll on the ground, and bite the furniture, was tearing at his entrails, and he felt inclined to take a knife and plunge it into his stomach. He started when he heard the door open. His wife came in. "I am hungry," she said; "are not you, Limousin?"

He hesitated a little, and then said: "Yes, I am, upon my word." She had the leg of mutton brought in again. Parent asked himself "Have they had dinner? Or are they late because they have had a lovers' meeting?"

They both ate with a very good appetite. Henriette was very calm, but laughed and joked. Her husband watched her furtively. She had on a pink teagown trimmed with white lace, and her fair head, her white neck and her plump hands stood out from that coquettish and perfumed dress as though it were a sea shell edged with foam.

What fun they must be making of him, if he had been their dupe since the first day! Was it possible to make a fool of a man, of a worthy man, because his father had left him a little money? Why could one not see into people's souls? How was it that nothing revealed to upright hearts the deceits of infamous hearts? How was it that voices had the same sound for adoring as for lying? Why was a false, deceptive look the same as a sincere one? And he watched them, waiting to catch a gesture, a word, an intonation. Then suddenly he thought: "I will surprise them this evening," and he said:

"My dear, as I have dismissed Julie, I will see about getting another girl this very day. I will go at once to procure one by to-morrow morning, so I may not be in until late."

"Very well," she replied; "go. I shall not stir from here. Limousin will keep me company. We will wait for you." Then, turning to the maid, she said: "You had better put George to bed, and then you can clear away and go up to your room."

Parent had got up; he was unsteady on his legs, dazed and bewildered, and saying, "I shall see you again later on," he went out, holding on to the wall, for the floor seemed to roll like a ship. George had been carried out by his nurse, while Henriette and Limousin went into the drawing-room.

As soon as the door was shut, he said: "You must be mad, surely, to torment your husband as you do?"

She immediately turned on him: "Ah! Do you know that I think the habit you have got into lately, of looking upon Parent as a martyr, is very unpleasant?"

Limousin threw himself into an easy-chair and crossed his legs. "I am not setting him up as a martyr in the least, but I think that, situated as we are, it is ridiculous to defy this man as you do, from morning till night."

She took a cigarette from the mantelpiece, lighted it, and replied: "But I do not defy him; quite the contrary. Only he irritates me by his stupidity, and I treat him as he deserves."

Limousin continued impatiently: "What you are doing is very foolish! I am only asking you to treat your husband gently, because we both of us require him to trust us. I think that you ought to see that."

They were close together: he, tall, dark, with long whiskers and the rather vulgar manners of a good-looking man who is very well satisfied with himself; she, small, fair, and pink, a little Parisian, born in the back room of a shop, half cocotte and half bourgeoise, brought up to entice customers to the store by her glances, and married, in consequence, to a simple, unsophisticated man, who saw her outside the door every morning when he went out and every evening when he came home.

"But do you not understand; you great booby," she said, "that I hate him just because he married me, because he bought me, in fact; because everything that he says and does, everything that he thinks, acts on my nerves? He exasperates me every moment by his stupidity, which you call his kindness; by his dullness, which you call his confidence, and then, above all, because he is my husband, instead of you. I feel him between us, although he does not interfere with us much. And then—-and then! No, it is, after all, too idiotic of him not to guess anything! I wish he would, at any rate, be a little jealous. There are moments when I feel inclined to say to him: 'Do you not see, you stupid creature, that Paul is my lover?'

"It is quite incomprehensible that you cannot understand how hateful he is to me, how he irritates me. You always seem to like him, and you shake hands with him cordially. Men are very extraordinary at times."

"One must know how to dissimulate, my dear."

"It is no question of dissimulation, but of feeling. One might think that, when you men deceive one another, you like each other better on that account, while we women hate a man from the moment that we have betrayed him."

"I do not see why one should hate an excellent fellow because one is friendly with his wife."

"You do not see it? You do not see it? You all of you are wanting in refinement of feeling. However, that is one of those things which one feels and cannot express. And then, moreover, one ought not. No, you would not understand; it is quite useless! You men have no delicacy of feeling."

And smiling, with the gentle contempt of an impure woman, she put both her hands on his shoulders and held up her lips to him. He stooped down and clasped her closely in his arms, and their lips met. And as they stood in front of the mantel mirror, another couple exactly like them embraced behind the clock.

They had heard nothing, neither the noise of the key nor the creaking of the door, but suddenly Henriette, with a loud cry, pushed Limousin away with both her arms, and they saw Parent looking at them, livid with rage, without his shoes on and his hat over his forehead. He looked at each, one after the other, with a quick glance of his eyes and without moving his head. He appeared beside himself. Then, without saying a word, he threw himself on Limousin, seized him as if he were going to strangle him, and flung him into the opposite corner of the room so violently that the other lost his balance, and, beating the air with his hand, struck his head violently against the wall.

When Henriette saw that her husband was going to murder her lover, she threw herself on Parent, seized him by the neck, and digging her ten delicate, rosy fingers into his neck, she squeezed him so tightly, with all the vigor of a desperate woman, that the blood spurted out under her nails, and she bit his shoulder, as if she wished to tear it with her teeth. Parent, half-strangled and choking, loosened his hold on Limousin, in order to shake off his wife, who was hanging to his neck. Putting his arms round her waist, he flung her also to the other end of the drawing-room.

Then, as his passion was short-lived, like that of most good-tempered men, and his strength was soon exhausted, he remained standing between the two, panting, worn out, not knowing what to do next. His brutal fury had expended itself in that effort, like the froth of a bottle of champagne, and his unwonted energy ended in a gasping for breath. As soon as he could speak, however, he said:

"Go away—both of you—immediately! Go away!"

Limousin remained motionless in his corner, against the wall, too startled to understand anything as yet, too frightened to move a finger; while Henriette, with her hands resting on a small, round table, her head bent forward, her hair hanging down, the bodice of her dress unfastened, waited like a wild animal which is about to spring. Parent continued in a stronger voice: "Go away immediately. Get out of the house!"

His wife, however, seeing that he had got over his first exasperation grew bolder, drew herself up, took two steps toward him, and, grown almost insolent, she said: "Have you lost your head? What is the matter with you? What is the meaning of this unjustifiable violence?"

But he turned toward her, and raising his fist to strike her, he stammered out: "Oh—oh—this is too much, too much! I heard everything! Everything—do you understand? Everything! You wretch—you wretch! You are two wretches! Get out of the house, both of you! Immediately, or I shall kill you! Leave the house!"

She saw that it was all over, and that he knew everything; that she could not prove her innocence, and that she must comply. But all her impudence had returned to her, and her hatred for the man, which was aggravated now, drove her to audacity, made her feel the need of bravado, and of defying him, and she said in a clear voice: "Come, Limousin; as he is going to turn me out of doors, I will go to your lodgings with you."

But Limousin did not move, and Parent, in a fresh access of rage, cried out: "Go, will you? Go, you wretches! Or else—or else——"
He seized a chair and whirled it over his head.

Henriette walked quickly across the room, took her lover by the arm, dragged him from the wall, to which he appeared fixed, and led him toward the door, saying: "Do come, my friend—you see that the man is mad. Do come!"

As she went out she turned round to her husband, trying to think of something that she could do, something that she could invent to wound him to the heart as she left the house, and an idea struck her, one of those venomous, deadly ideas in which all a woman's perfidy shows itself, and she said resolutely: "I am going to take my child with me."

Parent was stupefied, and stammered: "Your—your—child? You dare to talk of your child? You venture—you venture to ask for your child—after-after—Oh, oh, that is too much! Go, you vile creature! Go!"

She went up to him again, almost smiling, almost avenged already, and defying him, standing close to him, and face to face, she said: "I want my child, and you have no right to keep him, because he is not yours—do you understand? He is not yours! He is Limousin's!"

And Parent cried out in bewilderment: "You lie—you lie—worthless woman!"

But she continued: "You fool! Everybody knows it except you. I tell you, this is his father. You need only look at him to see it."

Parent staggered backward, and then he suddenly turned round, took a candle, and rushed into the next room; returning almost immediately, carrying little George wrapped up in his bedclothes. The child, who had been suddenly awakened, was crying from fright. Parent threw him into his wife's arms, and then, without speaking, he pushed her roughly out toward the stairs, where Limousin was waiting, from motives of prudence.

Then he shut the door again, double-locked and bolted it, but had scarcely got back into the drawing-room when he fell to the floor at full length.

Parent lived alone, quite alone. During the five weeks that followed their separation, the feeling of surprise at his new life prevented him from thinking much. He had resumed his bachelor life, his habits of lounging, about, and took his meals at a restaurant, as he had done formerly. As he wished to avoid any scandal, he made his wife an allowance, which was arranged by their lawyers. By degrees, however, the thought of the child began to haunt him. Often, when he was at home alone at night, he suddenly thought he heard George calling out "Papa," and his heart would begin to beat, and he would get up quickly and open the door, to see whether, by chance, the child might have returned, as dogs or pigeons do. Why should a child have less instinct than an animal? On finding that he was mistaken, he would sit down in his armchair again and think of the boy. He would think of him for hours and whole days. It was not only a moral, but still more a physical obsession, a nervous longing to kiss him, to hold and fondle him, to take him on his knees and dance him. He felt the child's little arms around his neck, his little mouth pressing a kiss on his beard, his soft hair tickling his cheeks, and the remembrance of all those childish ways made him suffer as a man might for some beloved woman who has left him. Twenty or a hundred times a day he asked himself the question whether he was or was not George's father, and almost before he was in bed every night he recommenced the same series of despairing questionings.

He especially dreaded the darkness of the evening, the melancholy feeling of the twilight. Then a flood of sorrow invaded his heart, a torrent of despair which seemed to overwhelm him and drive him mad. He was as afraid of his own thoughts as men are of criminals, and he fled before them as one does from wild beasts. Above all things, he feared his empty, dark, horrible dwelling and the deserted streets, in which, here and there, a gas lamp flickered, where the isolated foot passenger whom one hears in the distance seems to be a night prowler, and makes one walk faster or slower, according to whether he is coming toward you or following you.

And in spite of himself, and by instinct, Parent went in the direction of the broad, well-lighted, populous streets. The light and the crowd attracted him, occupied his mind and distracted his thoughts, and when he was tired of walking aimlessly about among the moving crowd, when he saw the foot passengers becoming more scarce and the pavements less crowded, the fear of solitude and silence drove him into some large cafe full of drinkers and of light. He went there as flies go to a candle, and he would sit down at one of the little round tables and ask for a "bock," which he would drink slowly, feeling uneasy every time a customer got up to go. He would have liked to take him by the arm, hold him back, and beg him to stay a little longer, so much did he dread the time when the waiter should come up to him and say sharply: "Come, monsieur, it is closing time!"

He thus got into the habit of going to the beer houses, where the continual elbowing of the drinkers brings you in contact with a familiar and silent public, where the heavy clouds of tobacco smoke lull disquietude, while the heavy beer dulls the mind and calms the heart. He almost lived there. He was scarcely up before he went there to find people to distract his glances and his thoughts, and soon, as he felt too lazy to move, he took his meals there.

After every meal, during more than an hour, he sipped three or four small glasses of brandy, which stupefied him by degrees, and then his head drooped on his chest, he shut his eyes, and went to sleep. Then, awaking, he raised himself on the red velvet seat, straightened his waistcoat, pulled down his cuffs, and took up the newspapers again, though he had already seen them in the morning, and read them all through again, from beginning to end. Between four and five o'clock he went for a walk on the boulevards, to get a little fresh air, as he used to say, and then came back to the seat which had been reserved for him, and asked for his absinthe. He would talk to the regular customers whose acquaintance he had made. They discussed the news of the day and political events, and that carried him on till dinner time; and he spent the evening as he had the afternoon, until it was time to close. That was a terrible moment for him when he was obliged to go out into the dark, into his empty room full of dreadful recollections, of horrible thoughts, and of mental agony. He no longer saw any of his old friends, none of his relatives, nobody who might remind him of his past life. But as his apartments were a hell to him, he took a room in a large hotel, a good room on the ground floor, so as to see the passers-by. He was no longer alone in that great building. He felt people swarming round him, he heard voices in the adjoining rooms, and when his former sufferings tormented him too much at the sight of his bed, which was turned down, and of his solitary fireplace, he went out into the wide passages and walked up and down them like a sentinel, before all the closed doors, and looked sadly at the shoes standing in couples outside them, women's little boots by the side of men's thick ones, and he thought that, no doubt, all these people were happy, and were sleeping in their warm beds. Five years passed thus; five miserable years. But one day, when he was taking his usual walk between the Madeleine and the Rue Drouot, he suddenly saw a lady whose bearing struck him. A tall gentleman and a child were with her, and all three were walking in front of him. He asked himself where he had seen them before, when suddenly he recognized a movement of her hand; it was his wife, his wife with Limousin and his child, his little George.

His heart beat as if it would suffocate him, but he did not stop, for he wished to see them, and he followed them. They looked like a family of the better middle class. Henriette was leaning on Paul's arm, and speaking to him in a low voice, and looking at him sideways occasionally. Parent got a side view of her and recognized her pretty features, the movements of her lips, her smile, and her coaxing glances. But the child chiefly took up his attention. How tall and strong he was! Parent could not see his face, but only his long, fair curls. That tall boy with bare legs, who was walking by his mother's side like a little man, was George. He saw them suddenly, all three, as they stopped in front of a shop. Limousin had grown very gray, had aged and was thinner; his wife, on the contrary, was as young looking as ever, and had grown stouter. George he would not have recognized, he was so different from what he had been formerly.

They went on again and Parent followed them. He walked on quickly, passed them, and then turned round, so as to meet them face to face. As he passed the child he felt a mad longing to take him into his arms and run off with him, and he knocked against him as if by accident. The boy turned round and looked at the clumsy man angrily, and Parent hurried away, shocked, hurt, and pursued by that look. He went off like a thief, seized with a horrible fear lest he should have been seen and recognized by his wife and her lover. He went to his cafe without stopping, and fell breathless into his chair. That evening he drank three absinthes. For four months he felt the pain of that meeting in his heart. Every night he saw the three again, happy and tranquil, father, mother, and child walking on the boulevard before going in to dinner, and that new vision effaced the old one. It was another matter, another hallucination now, and also a fresh pain. Little George, his little George, the child he had so much loved and so often kissed, disappeared in the far distance, and he saw a new one, like a brother of the first, a little boy with bare legs, who did not know him! He suffered terribly at that thought. The child's love was dead; there was no bond between them; the child would not have held out his arms when he saw him. He had even looked at him angrily.

Then, by degrees he grew calmer, his mental torture diminished, the image that had appeared to his eyes and which haunted his nights became more indistinct and less frequent. He began once more to live nearly like everybody else, like all those idle people who drink beer off marble-topped tables and wear out their clothes on the threadbare velvet of the couches.

He grew old amid the smoke from pipes, lost his hair under the gas lights, looked upon his weekly bath, on his fortnightly visit to the barber's to have his hair cut, and on the purchase of a new coat or hat as an event. When he got to his cafe in a new hat he would look at himself in the glass for a long time before sitting down, and take it off and put it on again several times, and at last ask his friend, the lady at the bar, who was watching him with interest, whether she thought it suited him.

Two or three times a year he went to the theatre, and in the summer he sometimes spent his evenings at one of the open-air concerts in the Champs Elysees. And so the years followed each other slow, monotonous, and short, because they were quite uneventful.

He very rarely now thought of the dreadful drama which had wrecked his life; for twenty years had passed since that terrible evening. But the life he had led since then had worn him out. The landlord of his cafe would often say to him: "You ought to pull yourself together a little, Monsieur Parent; you should get some fresh air and go into the country. I assure you that you have changed very much within the last few months." And when his customer had gone out be used to say to the barmaid: "That poor Monsieur Parent is booked for another world; it is bad never to get out of Paris. Advise him to go out of town for a day occasionally; he has confidence in you. Summer will soon be here; that will put him straight."

And she, full of pity and kindness for such a regular customer, said to Parent every day: "Come, monsieur, make up your mind to get a little fresh air. It is so charming in the country when the weather is fine. Oh, if I could, I would spend my life there!"

By degrees he was seized with a vague desire to go just once and see whether it was really as pleasant there as she said, outside the walls of the great city. One morning he said to her:

"Do you know where one can get a good luncheon in the neighborhood of Paris?"

"Go to the Terrace at Saint-Germain; it is delightful there!"

He had been there formerly, just when he became engaged. He made up his mind to go there again, and he chose a Sunday, for no special reason, but merely because people generally do go out on Sundays, even when they have nothing to do all the week; and so one Sunday morning he went to Saint-Germain. He felt low-spirited and vexed at having yielded to that new longing, and at having broken through his usual habits. He was thirsty; he would have liked to get out at every station and sit down in the cafe which he saw outside and drink a "bock" or two, and then take the first train back to Paris. The journey seemed very long to him. He could remain sitting for whole days, as long as he had the same motionless objects before his eyes, but he found it very trying and fatiguing to remain sitting while he was being whirled along, and to see the whole country fly by, while he himself was motionless.

However, he found the Seine interesting every time he crossed it. Under the bridge at Chatou he saw some small boats going at great speed under the vigorous strokes of the bare-armed oarsmen, and he thought: "There are some fellows who are certainly enjoying themselves!" The train entered the tunnel just before you get to the station at Saint-Germain, and presently stopped at the platform. Parent got out, and walked slowly, for he already felt tired, toward the Terrace, with his hands behind his back, and when he got to the iron balustrade, stopped to look at the distant horizon. The immense plain spread out before him vast as the sea, green and studded with large villages, almost as populous as towns. The sun bathed the whole landscape in its full, warm light. The Seine wound like an endless serpent through the plain, flowed round the villages and along the slopes. Parent inhaled the warm breeze, which seemed to make his heart young again, to enliven his spirits, and to vivify his blood, and said to himself:

"Why, it is delightful here."

Then he went on a few steps, and stopped again to look about him. The utter misery of his existence seemed to be brought into full relief by the intense light which inundated the landscape. He saw his twenty years of cafe life—dull, monotonous, heartbreaking. He might have traveled as others did, have gone among foreigners, to unknown countries beyond the sea, have interested himself somewhat in everything which other men are passionately devoted to, in arts and science; he might have enjoyed life in a thousand forms, that mysterious life which is either charming or painful, constantly changing, always inexplicable and strange. Now, however, it was too late. He would go on drinking "bock" after "bock" until he died, without any family, without friends, without hope, without any curiosity about anything, and he was seized with a feeling of misery and a wish to run away, to hide himself in Paris, in his cafe and his lethargy! All the thoughts, all the dreams, all the desires which are dormant in the slough of stagnating hearts had reawakened, brought to life by those rays of sunlight on the plain.

Parent felt that if he were to remain there any longer he should lose his reason, and he made haste to get to the Pavilion Henri IV for lunch, to try and forget his troubles under—the influence of wine and alcohol, and at any rate to have some one to speak to.

He took a small table in one of the arbors, from which one can see all the surrounding country, ordered his lunch, and asked to be served at once. Then some more people arrived and sat down at tables near him. He felt more comfortable; he was no longer alone. Three persons were eating luncheon near him. He looked at them two or three times without seeing them clearly, as one looks at total strangers. Suddenly a woman's voice sent a shiver through him which seemed to penetrate to his very marrow. "George," it said, "will you carve the chicken?"

And another voice replied: "Yes, mamma."

Parent looked up, and he understood; he guessed immediately who those people were! He should certainly not have known them again. His wife had grown quite white and very stout, an elderly, serious, respectable lady, and she held her head forward as she ate for fear of spotting her dress, although she had a table napkin tucked under her chin. George had become a man. He had a slight beard, that uneven and almost colorless beard which adorns the cheeks of youths. He wore a high hat, a white waistcoat, and a monocle, because it looked swell, no doubt. Parent looked at him in astonishment. Was that George, his son? No, he did not know that young man; there could be nothing in common between them. Limousin had his back to him, and was eating, with his shoulders rather bent.

All three of them seemed happy and satisfied; they came and took luncheon in the country at well-known restaurants. They had had a calm and pleasant existence, a family existence in a warm and comfortable house, filled with all those trifles which make life agreeable, with affection, with all those tender words which people exchange continually when they love each other. They had lived thus, thanks to him, Parent, on his money, after having deceived him, robbed him, ruined him! They had condemned him, the innocent, simple-minded, jovial man, to all the miseries of solitude, to that abominable life which he had led, between the pavement and a bar-room, to every mental torture and every physical misery! They had made him a useless, aimless being, a waif in the world, a poor old man without any pleasures, any prospects, expecting nothing from anybody or anything. For him, the world was empty, because he loved nothing in the world. He might go among other nations, or go about the streets, go into all the houses in Paris, open every room, but he would not find inside any door the beloved face, the face of wife or child which smiles when it sees you. This idea worked upon him more than any other, the idea of a door which one opens, to see and to embrace somebody behind it.

And that was the fault of those three wretches! The fault of that worthless woman, of that infamous friend, and of that tall, light-haired lad who put on insolent airs. Now he felt as angry with the child as he did with the other two. Was he not Limousin's son? Would Limousin have kept him and loved him otherwise? Would not Limousin very quickly have got rid of the mother and of the child if he had not felt sure that it was his, positively his? Does anybody bring up other people's children? And now they were there, quite close to him, those three who had made him suffer so much.

Parent looked at them, irritated and excited at the recollection of all his sufferings and of his despair, and was especially exasperated at their placid and satisfied looks. He felt inclined to kill them, to throw his siphon of Seltzer water at them, to split open Limousin's head as he every moment bent it over his plate, raising it again immediately.

He would have his revenge now, on the spot, as he had them under his hand. But how? He tried to think of some means, he pictured such dreadful things as one reads of in the newspapers occasionally, but could not hit on anything practical. And he went on drinking to excite himself, to give himself courage not to allow such an opportunity to escape him, as he might never have another.

Suddenly an idea struck him, a terrible idea; and he left off drinking to mature it. He smiled as he murmured: "I have them, I have them! We will see; we will see!"

They finished their luncheon slowly, conversing with perfect unconcern. Parent could not hear what they were saying, but he saw their quiet gestures. His wife's face especially exasperated him. She had assumed a haughty air, the air of a comfortable, devout woman, of an unapproachable, devout woman, sheathed in principles, iron-clad in virtue. They paid their bill and got up from table. Parent then noticed Limousin. He might have been taken for a retired diplomat, for he looked a man of great importance, with his soft white whiskers, the tips of which touched his coat collar.

They walked away. Parent rose and followed them. First they went up and down the terrace, and calmly admired the landscape, and then they went into the forest. Parent followed them at a distance, hiding himself so as not to excite their suspicion too soon.

Parent came up to them by degrees, breathing hard with emotion and fatigue, for he was unused to walking now. He soon came up to them, but was seized with fear, an inexplicable fear, and he passed them, so as to turn round and meet them face to face. He walked on, his heart beating, feeling that they were just behind him now, and he said to himself: "Come, now is the time. Courage! courage! Now is the moment!"

He turned round. They were all three sitting on the grass, at the foot of a huge tree, and were still chatting. He made up his mind, and walked back rapidly; stopping in front of them in the middle of the road, he said abruptly, in a voice broken by emotion:

"It is I! Here I am! I suppose you did not expect me?"

They all three stared at this man, who seemed to be insane. He continued:

"One would suppose that you did not know me again. Just look at me! I am Parent, Henri Parent. You thought it was all over, and that you would never see me again. Ah! but here I am once more, you see, and now we will have an explanation."

Henriette, terrified, hid her face in her hands, murmuring: "Oh! Good heavens!"

Seeing this stranger, who seemed to be threatening his mother, George sprang up, ready to seize him by the collar. Limousin, thunderstruck, looked in horror at this apparition, who, after gasping for breath, continued:

"So now we will have an explanation; the proper moment has come! Ah! you deceived me, you condemned me to the life of a convict, and you thought that I should never catch you!"

The young man took him by the shoulders and pushed him back.

"Are you mad?" he asked. "What do you want? Go on your way immediately, or I shall give you a thrashing!"

"What do I want?" replied Parent. "I want to tell you who these people are."

George, however, was in a rage, and shook him; and was even going to strike him.

"Let me go," said Parent. "I am your father. There, see whether they recognize me now, the wretches!"

The young man, thunderstruck, unclenched his fists and turned toward his mother. Parent, as soon as he was released, approached her.

"Well," he said, "tell him yourself who I am! Tell him that my name is Henri Parent, that I am his father because his name is George Parent, because you are my wife, because you are all three living on my money, on the allowance of ten thousand francs which I have made you since I drove you out of my house. Will you tell him also why I drove you out? Because I surprised you

Guy de Maupassant

with this beggar, this wretch, your lover! Tell him what I was, an honorable man, whom you married for money, and whom you deceived from the very first day. Tell him who you are, and who I am——"

He stammered and gasped for breath in his rage. The woman exclaimed in a heartrending voice:

"Paul, Paul, stop him; make him be quiet! Do not let him say this before my son!"

Limousin had also risen to his feet. He said in a very low voice: "Hold your tongue! Hold your tongue! Do you understand what you are doing?"

"I quite know what I am doing," resumed Parent, "and that is not all. There is one thing that I will know, something that has tormented me for twenty years." Then, turning to George, who was leaning against a tree in consternation, he said:

"Listen to me. When she left my house she thought it was not enough to have deceived me, but she also wanted to drive me to despair. You were my only consolation, and she took you with her, swearing that I was not your father, but, that he was your father. Was she lying? I do not know. I have been asking myself the question for the last twenty years." He went close up to her, tragic and terrible, and, pulling away her hands, with which she had covered her face, he continued:

"Well, now! I call upon you to tell me which of us two is the father of this young man; he or I, your husband or your lover. Come! Come! tell us."

Limousin rushed at him. Parent pushed him back, and, sneering in his fury, he said: "Ah! you are brave now! You are braver than you were that day when you ran downstairs because you thought I was going to murder you. Very well! If she will not reply, tell me yourself. You ought to know as well as she. Tell me, are you this young fellow's father? Come! Come! Tell me!"

He turned to his wife again. "If you will not tell me, at any rate tell your son. He is a man, now, and he has the right to know who his father is. I do not know, and I never did know, never, never! I cannot tell you, my boy."

He seemed to be losing his senses; his voice grew shrill and he worked his arms about as if he had an epileptic 'fit.

"Come! . . . Give me an answer. She does not know . . . I will make a bet that she does not know . . . No . . . she does not know, by Jove! Ha! ha! ha! Nobody knows . . . nobody . . . How can one know such things?

"You will not know either, my boy, you will not know any more than I do . . . never. . . . Look here . . . Ask her you will find that she does not know . . . I do not know either . . . nor does he, nor do you, nobody knows. You can choose . . . You can choose . . . yes, you can choose him or me. . . Choose.

"Good evening . . . It is all over. If she makes up her mind to tell you, you will come and let me know, will you not? I am living at the Hotel des Continents . . . I should be glad to know . . . Good evening . . . I hope you will enjoy yourselves very much . . ."

And he went away gesticulating, talking to himself under the tall trees, in the quiet, the cool air, which was full of the fragrance of growing plants. He did not turn round to look at them, but went straight on, walking under the stimulus of his rage, under a storm of passion, with that one fixed idea in his mind. All at once he found himself outside the station. A train was about to start and he got in. During the journey his anger calmed down, he regained his senses and returned to Paris, astonished at his own boldness, full of aches and pains as if he had broken some bones. Nevertheless, he went to have a "bock" at his brewery.

When she saw him come in, Mademoiselle Zoe asked in surprise: "What! back already? are you tired?"

"Yes—yes, I am tired . . . very tired . . . You know, when one is not used to going out. . . I've had enough of it. I shall not go into the country again. It would have been better to have stayed here. For the future, I shall not stir out."

She could not persuade him to tell her about his little excursion, much as she wished to.

For the first time in his life he got thoroughly drunk that night, and had to be carried home.

QUEEN HORTENSE

In Argenteuil she was called Queen Hortense. No one knew why. Perhaps it was because she had a commanding tone of voice; perhaps because she was tall, bony, imperious; perhaps because she governed a kingdom of servants, chickens, dogs, cats, canaries, parrots, all so dear to an old maid's heart. But she did not spoil these familiar friends; she had for them none of those endearing names, none of the foolish tenderness which women seem to lavish on the soft fur of a purring cat. She governed these beasts with authority; she reigned.

She was indeed an old maid—one of those old maids with a harsh voice and angular motions, whose very soul seems to be hard. She never would stand contradiction, argument, hesitation, indifference, laziness nor fatigue. She had never been heard to complain, to regret anything, to envy anyone. She would say: "Everyone has his share," with the conviction of a fatalist. She did not go to church, she had no use for priests, she hardly believed in God, calling all religious things "weeper's wares."

For thirty years she had lived in her little house, with its tiny garden running along the street; she had never changed her habits, only changing her servants pitilessly, as soon as they reached twenty-one years of age.

When her dogs, cats and birds would die of old age, or from an accident, she would replace them without tears and without regret; with a little spade she would bury the dead animal in a strip of ground, throwing a few shovelfuls of earth over it and stamping it down with her feet in an indifferent manner.

She had a few friends in town, families of clerks who went to Paris every day. Once in a while she would be invited out, in the evening, to tea. She would inevitably fall asleep, and she would have to be awakened, when it was time for her to go home. She never allowed anyone to accompany her, fearing neither light nor darkness. She did not appear to like children.

She kept herself busy doing countless masculine tasks—carpentering, gardening, sawing or chopping wood, even laying bricks when it was necessary.

She had relatives who came to see her twice a year, the Cimmes and the Colombels, her two sisters having married, one of them a florist and the other a retired merchant. The Cimmes had no children; the Colombels had three: Henri, Pauline and Joseph. Henri was twenty, Pauline seventeen and Joseph only three.

There was no love lost between the old maid and her relatives.

In the spring of the year 1882 Queen Hortense suddenly fell sick. The neighbors called in a physician, whom she immediately drove out. A priest then having presented himself, she jumped out of bed, in order to throw him out of the house.

The young servant, in despair, was brewing her some tea.

After lying in bed for three days the situation appeared so serious that the barrel-maker, who lived next door, to the right, acting on advice from the doctor, who had forcibly returned to the house, took it upon himself to call together the two families.

They arrived by the same train, towards ten in the morning, the Colombels bringing little Joseph with them.

When they got to the garden gate, they saw the servant seated in the chair against the wall, crying.

The dog was sleeping on the door mat in the broiling sun; two cats, which looked as though they might be dead, were stretched out in front of the two windows, their eyes closed, their paws and tails stretched out at full length.

A big clucking hen was parading through the garden with a whole regiment of yellow, downy chicks, and a big cage hanging from the wall and covered with pimpernel, contained a population of birds which were chirping away in the warmth of this beautiful spring morning.

In another cage, shaped like a chalet, two lovebirds sat motionless side by side on their perch.

M. Cimme, a fat, puffing person, who always entered first everywhere, pushing aside everyone else, whether man or woman, when it was necessary, asked:

"Well, Celeste, aren't things going well?"

The little servant moaned through her tears:

"She doesn't even recognize me any more. The doctor says it's the end."

Everybody looked around.

Mme. Cimme and Mme. Colombel immediately embraced each other, without saying a word. They looked very much alike, having always worn their hair in Madonna bands, and loud red French cashmere shawls.

Cimme turned to his brother-in-law, a pale, sallow-complexioned, thin man, wasted by stomach complaints, who limped badly, and said in a serious tone of voice:

"Gad! It was high time."

But no one dared to enter the dying woman's room on the ground floor. Even Cimme made way for the others. Colombel was the first to make up his mind, and, swaying from side to side like the mast of a ship, the iron ferule of his cane clattering on the paved hall, he entered.

The two women were the next to venture, and M. Cimmes closed the procession.

Little Joseph had remained outside, pleased at the sight of the dog.

A ray of sunlight seemed to cut the bed in two, shining just on the hands, which were moving nervously, continually opening and closing. The fingers were twitching as though moved by some thought, as though trying to point out a meaning or idea, as though obeying the dictates of a will. The rest of the body lay motionless under the sheets. The angular frame showed not a single movement. The eyes remained closed.

The family spread out in a semi-circle and, without a word, they began to watch the contracted chest and the short, gasping breathing. The little servant had followed them and was still crying.

At last Cimme asked:

"Exactly what did the doctor say?"

The girl stammered:

"He said to leave her alone, that nothing more could be done for her."

But suddenly the old woman's lips began to move. She seemed to be uttering silent words, words hidden in the brain of this dying being, and her hands quickened their peculiar movements.

Then she began to speak in a thin, high voice, which no one had ever heard, a voice which seemed to come from the distance, perhaps from the depths of this heart which had always been closed.

Cimme, finding this scene painful, walked away on tiptoe. Colombel, whose crippled leg was growing tired, sat down.

The two women remained standing.

Queen Hortense was now babbling away, and no one could understand a word. She was pronouncing names, many names, tenderly calling imaginary people.

"Come here, Philippe, kiss your mother. Tell me, child, do you love your mamma? You, Rose, take care of your little sister while

I am away. And don't leave her alone. Don't play with matches!"

She stopped for a while, then, in a louder voice, as though she were calling someone: "Henriette!" then waited a moment and continued:

"Tell your father that I wish to speak to him before he goes to business." And suddenly: "I am not feeling very well to-day, darling; promise not to come home late. Tell your employer that I am sick. You know, it isn't safe to leave the children alone when I am in bed. For dinner I will fix you up a nice dish of rice. The little ones like that very much. Won't Claire be happy?"

And she broke into a happy, joyous laugh, such as they had never heard: "Look at Jean, how funny he looks! He has smeared jam all over his face, the little pig! Look, sweetheart, look; isn't he funny?"

Colombel, who was continually lifting his tired leg from place to place, muttered:

"She is dreaming that she has children and a husband; it is the beginning of the death agony."

The two sisters had not yet moved, surprised, astounded.

The little maid exclaimed:

"You must take off your shawls and your hats! Would you like to go into the parlor?"

They went out without having said a word. And Colombel followed them, limping, once more leaving the dying woman alone.

When they were relieved of their travelling garments, the women finally sat down. Then one of the cats left its window, stretched, jumped into the room and on to Mme. Cimme's knees. She began to pet it.

In the next room could be heard the voice of the dying woman, living, in this last hour, the life for which she had doubtless hoped, living her dreams themselves just when all was over for her.

Cimme, in the garden, was playing with little Joseph and the dog, enjoying himself in the whole hearted manner of a countryman, having completely forgotten the dying woman.

But suddenly he entered the house and said to the girl:

"I say, my girl, are we not going to have luncheon? What do you ladies wish to eat?"

They finally agreed on an omelet, a piece of steak with new potatoes, cheese and coffee.

As Mme. Colombel was fumbling in her pocket for her purse, Cimme stopped her, and, turning to the maid: "Have you got any money?"

She answered:

"Yes, monsieur."

"How much?"

"Fifteen francs."

"That's enough. Hustle, my girl, because I am beginning to get very hungry."

Mme. Cimme, looking out over the climbing vines bathed in sunlight, and at the two turtle-doves on the roof opposite, said in an annoyed tone of voice:

"What a pity to have had to come for such a sad occasion. It is so nice in the country to-day."

Her sister sighed without answering, and Colombel mumbled, thinking perhaps of the walk ahead of him:

"My leg certainly is bothering me to-day."

Little Joseph and the dog were making a terrible noise; one was shrieking with pleasure, the other was barking wildly. They were playing hide-and-seek around the three flower beds, running after each other like mad.

The dying woman continued to call her children, talking with each one, imagining that she was dressing them, fondling them, teaching them how to read: "Come on! Simon repeat: A, B, C, D. You are not paying attention, listen—D, D, D; do you hear me? Now repeat—"

Cimme exclaimed: "Funny what people say when in that condition."

Mme. Colombel then asked:

"Wouldn't it be better if we were to return to her?"

But Cimme dissuaded her from the idea:

"What's the use? You can't change anything. We are just as comfortable here."

Nobody insisted. Mme. Cimme observed the two green birds called love-birds. In a few words she praised this singular faithfulness and blamed the men for not imitating these animals. Cimme began to laugh, looked at his wife and hummed in a teasing way: "Tra-la-la, tra-la-la" as though to cast a good deal of doubt on his own, Cimme's, faithfulness.

Colombel was suffering from cramps and was rapping the floor with his cane.

The other cat, its tail pointing upright to the sky, now came in.

They sat down to luncheon at one o'clock.

As soon as he had tasted the wine, Colombel, for whom only the best of Bordeaux had been prescribed, called the servant back:

"I say, my girl, is this the best stuff that you have in the cellar?"

"No, monsieur; there is some better wine, which was only brought out when you came."

"Well, bring us three bottles of it."

They tasted the wine and found it excellent, not because it was of a remarkable vintage, but because it had been in the cellar fifteen years. Cimme declared:

"That is regular invalid's wine."

Colombel, filled with an ardent desire to gain possession of this Bordeaux, once more questioned the girl:

"How much of it is left?"

"Oh! Almost all, monsieur; mamz'elle never touched it. It's in the bottom stack."

Then he turned to his brother-in-law:

"If you wish, Cimme, I would be willing to exchange something else for this wine; it suits my stomach marvellously."

The chicken had now appeared with its regiment of young ones. The two women were enjoying themselves throwing crumbs to them.

Joseph and the dog, who had eaten enough, were sent back to the garden.

Queen Hortense was still talking, but in a low, hushed voice, so that the words could no longer be distinguished.

When they had finished their coffee all went in to observe the condition of the sick woman. She seemed calm.

They went outside again and seated themselves in a circle in the garden, in order to complete their digestion.

Suddenly the dog, who was carrying something in his mouth, began to run around the chairs at full speed. The child was chasing him wildly. Both disappeared into the house.

Cimme fell asleep, his well-rounded paunch bathed in the glow of the shining sun.

The dying woman once more began to talk in a loud voice. Then suddenly she shrieked.

The two women and Colombel rushed in to see what was the matter. Cimme, waking up, did not budge, because, he did not wish to witness such a scene.

She was sitting up, with haggard eyes. Her dog, in order to escape being pursued by little Joseph, had jumped up on the bed, run over the sick woman, and entrenched behind the pillow, was looking down at his playmate with snapping eyes, ready to jump down and begin the game again. He was holding in his mouth one of his mistress' slippers, which he had torn to pieces and with which he had been playing for the last hour.

The child, frightened by this woman who had suddenly risen in front of him, stood motionless before the bed.

The hen had also come in, and frightened by the noise, had jumped up on a chair and was wildly calling her chicks, who were chirping distractedly around the four legs of the chair.

Queen Hortense was shrieking:

"No, no, I don't want to die, I don't want to! I don't want to! Who will bring up my children? Who will take care of them? Who will love them? No, I don't want to!—I don't——"

She fell back. All was over.

The dog, wild with excitement, jumped about the room, barking.

Colombel ran to the window, calling his brother-in-law:

"Hurry up, hurry up! I think that she has just gone."

Then Cimme, resigned, arose and entered the room, mumbling "It didn't take as long as I thought it would!"

TIMBUCTOO

The boulevard, that river of humanity, was alive with people in the golden light of the setting sun. The whole sky was red, blinding, and behind the Madeleine an immense bank of flaming clouds cast a shower of light the whole length of the boulevard, vibrant as the heat from a brazier.

The gay, animated crowd went by in this golden mist and seemed to be glorified. Their faces were gilded, their black hats and clothes took on purple tints, the patent leather of their shoes cast bright reflections on the asphalt of the sidewalk.

Before the cafes a mass of men were drinking opalescent liquids that looked like precious stones dissolved in the glasses.

In the midst of the drinkers two officers in full uniform dazzled all eyes with their glittering gold lace. They chatted, happy without asking why, in this glory of life, in this radiant light of sunset, and they looked at the crowd, the leisurely men and the hurrying women who left a bewildering odor of perfume as they passed by.

All at once an enormous negro, dressed in black, with a paunch beneath his jean waistcoat, which was covered with charms, his face shining as if it had been polished, passed before them with a triumphant air. He laughed at the passers-by, at the news venders, at the dazzling sky, at the whole of Paris. He was so tall that he overtopped everyone else, and when he passed all the loungers turned round to look at his back.

But he suddenly perceived the officers and darted towards them, jostling the drinkers in his path. As soon as he reached their table he fixed his gleaming and delighted eyes upon them and the corners of his mouth expanded to his ears, showing his dazzling white teeth like a crescent moon in a black sky. The two men looked in astonishment at this ebony giant, unable to understand his delight.

With a voice that made all the guests laugh, he said:

"Good-day, my lieutenant."

One of the officers was commander of a battalion, the other was a colonel. The former said:

"I do not know you, sir. I am at a loss to know what you want of me."

"Me like you much, Lieutenant Vedie, siege of Bezi, much grapes, find me."

The officer, utterly bewildered, looked at the man intently, trying to refresh his memory. Then he cried abruptly:

"Timbuctoo?"

The negro, radiant, slapped his thigh as he uttered a tremendous laugh and roared:

"Yes, yes, my lieutenant; you remember Timbuctoo, ya. How do you do?"

The commandant held out his hand, laughing heartily as he did so. Then Timbuctoo became serious. He seized the officer's hand and, before the other could prevent it, he kissed it, according to negro and Arab custom. The officer embarrassed, said in a severe tone:

"Come now, Timbuctoo, we are not in Africa. Sit down there and tell me how it is I find you here."

Timbuctoo swelled himself out and, his words falling over one another, replied hurriedly:

"Make much money, much, big restaurant, good food; Prussians, me, much steal, much, French cooking; Timbuctoo cook to the emperor; two thousand francs mine. Ha, ha, ha, ha!"

And he laughed, doubling himself up, roaring, with wild delight in his glances.

When the officer, who understood his strange manner of expressing himself, had questioned him he said:

"Well, au revoir, Timbuctoo. I will see you again."

The negro rose, this time shaking the hand that was extended to him and, smiling still, cried:

"Good-day, good-day, my lieutenant!"

He went off so happy that he gesticulated as he walked, and people thought he was crazy.

"Who is that brute?" asked the colonel.

"A fine fellow and a brave soldier. I will tell you what I know about him. It is funny enough.

"You know that at the commencement of the war of 1870 I was shut up in Bezieres, that this negro calls Bezi. We were not besieged, but blockaded. The Prussian lines surrounded us on all sides, outside the reach of cannon, not firing on us, but slowly starving us out.

"I was then lieutenant. Our garrison consisted of soldier of all descriptions, fragments of slaughtered regiments, some that had run away, freebooters separated from the main army, etc. We had all kinds, in fact even eleven Turcos [Algerian soldiers in the service of France], who arrived one evening no one knew whence or how. They appeared at the gates of the city, exhausted, in rags, starving and dirty. They were handed over to me.

"I saw very soon that they were absolutely undisciplined, always in the street and always drunk. I tried putting them in the police station, even in prison, but nothing was of any use. They would disappear, sometimes for days at a time, as if they had been swallowed up by the earth, and then come back staggering drunk. They had no money. Where did they buy drink and how and with what?

"This began to worry me greatly, all the more as these savages interested me with their everlasting laugh and their characteristics of overgrown frolicsome children.

"I then noticed that they blindly obeyed the largest among them, the one you have just seen. He made them do as he pleased, planned their mysterious expeditions with the all-powerful and undisputed authority of a leader. I sent for him and questioned him. Our conversation lasted fully three hours, for it was hard for me to understand his remarkable gibberish. As for him, poor devil, he made unheard-of efforts to make himself intelligible, invented words, gesticulated, perspired in his anxiety, mopping his forehead, puffing, stopping and abruptly beginning again when he thought he had found a new method of explaining what he wanted to say.

"I gathered finally that he was the son of a big chief, a sort of negro king of the region around Timbuctoo. I asked him his name. He repeated something like 'Chavaharibouhalikranafotapolara.' It seemed simpler to me to give him the name of his native place, 'Timbuctoo.' And a week later he was known by no other name in the garrison.

"But we were all wildly anxious to find out where this African ex-prince procured his drinks. I discovered it in a singular manner.

"I was on the ramparts one morning, watching the horizon, when I perceived something moving about in a vineyard. It was near the time of vintage, the grapes were ripe, but I was not thinking of that. I thought that a spy was approaching the town, and I organized a complete expedition to catch the prowler. I took command myself, after obtaining permission from the general.

"I sent out by three different gates three little companies, which were to meet at the suspected vineyard and form a cordon round it. In order to cut off the spy's retreat, one of these detachments had to make at least an hour's march. A watch on the walls signalled to me that the person I had seen had not left the place. We went along in profound silence, creeping, almost crawling, along the ditches. At last we reached the spot assigned.

"I abruptly disbanded my soldiers, who darted into the vineyard and found Timbuctoo on hands and knees travelling around among the vines and eating grapes, or rather devouring them as a dog eats his sop, snatching them in mouthfuls from the vine with his teeth.

"I wanted him to get up, but he could not think of it. I then understood why he was crawling on his hands and knees. As soon as we stood him on his feet he began to wabble, then stretched out his arms and fell down on his nose. He was more drunk than I have ever seen anyone.

"They brought him home on two poles. He never stopped laughing all the way back, gesticulating with his arms and legs.

"This explained the mystery. My men also drank the juice of the grapes, and when they were so intoxicated they could not stir they went to sleep in the vineyard. As for Timbuctoo, his love of the vineyard was beyond all belief and all bounds. He lived in it as did the thrushes, whom he hated with the jealous hate of a rival. He repeated incessantly: 'The thrushes eat all the grapes, captain!'

"One evening I was sent for. Something had been seen on the plain coming in our direction. I had not brought my field-glass and I could not distinguish things clearly. It looked like a great serpent uncoiling itself—a convoy. How could I tell?

"I sent some men to meet this strange caravan, which presently made its triumphal entry. Timbuctoo and nine of his comrades were carrying on a sort of altar made of camp stools eight severed, grinning and bleeding heads. The African was dragging along a horse to whose tail another head was fastened, and six other animals followed, adorned in the same manner.

"This is what I learned: Having started out to the vineyard, my Africans had suddenly perceived a detachment of Prussians approaching a village. Instead of taking to their heels, they hid themselves, and as soon as the Prussian officers dismounted at an inn to refresh themselves, the eleven rascals rushed on them, put to flight the lancers, who thought they were being attacked by the main army, killed the two sentries, then the colonel and the five officers of his escort.

"That day I kissed Timbuctoo. I saw, however, that he walked with difficulty and thought he was wounded. He laughed and said:

"'Me provisions for my country.'

"Timbuctoo was not fighting for glory, but for gain. Everything he found that seemed to him to be of the slightest value, especially anything that glistened, he put in his pocket. What a pocket! An abyss that began at his hips and reached to his ankles. He had retained an old term used by the troopers and called it his 'profonde,' and it was his 'profonde' in fact.

"He had taken the gold lace off the Prussian uniforms, the brass off their helmets, detached their buttons, etc., and had thrown them all into his 'profonde,' which was full to overflowing.

"Each day he pocketed every glistening object that came beneath his observation, pieces of tin or pieces of silver, and sometimes his contour was very comical.

"He intended to carry all that back to the land of ostriches, whose brother he might have been, this son of a king, tormented with the longing to gobble up all objects that glistened. If he had not had his 'profonde' what would he have done? He doubtless would have swallowed them.

"Each morning his pocket was empty. He had, then, some general store where his riches were piled up. But where? I could not discover it.

"The general, on being informed of Timbuctoo's mighty act of valor, had the headless bodies that had been left in the neighboring village interred at once, that it might not be discovered that they were decapitated. The Prussians returned thither the following day. The mayor and seven prominent inhabitants were shot on the spot, by way of reprisal, as having denounced the Prussians.

"Winter was here. We were exhausted and desperate. There were skirmishes now every day. The famished men could no longer march. The eight 'Turcos' alone (three had been killed) remained fat and shiny, vigorous and always ready to fight. Timbuctoo was even getting fatter. He said to me one day:

"'You much hungry; me good meat.'

"And he brought me an excellent filet. But of what? We had no more cattle, nor sheep, nor goats, nor donkeys, nor pigs. It was impossible to get a horse. I thought of all this after I had devoured my meat. Then a horrible idea came to me. These negroes were born close to a country where they eat human beings! And each day such a number of soldiers were killed around the town! I questioned Timbuctoo. He would not answer. I did not insist, but from that time on I declined his presents.

"He worshipped me. One night snow took us by surprise at the outposts. We were seated, on the ground. I looked with pity at those poor negroes shivering beneath this white frozen shower. I was very cold and began to cough. At once I felt something fall on me like a large warm quilt. It was Timbuctoo's cape that he had thrown on my shoulders.

"I rose and returned his garment, saying:

"'Keep it, my boy; you need it more than I do.'

"'Non, my lieutenant, for you; me no need. Me hot, hot!'

"And he looked at me entreatingly.

"'Come, obey orders. Keep your cape; I insist,' I replied.

"He then stood up, drew his sword, which he had sharpened to an edge like a scythe, and holding in his other hand the large cape which I had refused, said:

"'If you not keep cape, me cut. No one cape.'

"And he would have done it. So I yielded.

"Eight days later we capitulated. Some of us had been able to escape, the rest were to march out of the town and give themselves up to the conquerors.

"I went towards the exercising ground, where we were all to meet, when I was dumfounded at the sight of a gigantic negro dressed in white duck and wearing a straw hat. It was Timbuctoo. He was beaming and was walking with his hands in his pockets in front of a little shop where two plates and two glasses were displayed.

"'What are you doing?' I said.

"'Me not go. Me good cook; me make food for Colonel Algeria. Me eat Prussians; much steal, much.'

"There were ten degrees of frost. I shivered at sight of this negro in white duck. He took me by the arm and made me go inside. I noticed an immense flag that he was going to place outside his door as soon as we had left, for he had some shame."

I read this sign, traced by the hand of some accomplice

"'ARMY KITCHEN OF M. TIMBUCTOO,

"'Formerly Cook to H. M. the Emperor.

"'A Parisian Artist. Moderate Prices.'

"In spite of the despair that was gnawing at my heart, I could not help laughing, and I left my negro to his new enterprise.

"Was not that better than taking him prisoner?

"You have just seen that he made a success of it, the rascal.

"Bezieres to-day belongs to the Germans. The 'Restaurant Timbuctoo' is the beginning of a retaliation."

TOMBSTONES

The five friends had finished dinner, five men of the world, mature, rich, three married, the two others bachelors. They met like this every month in memory of their youth, and after dinner they chatted until two o'clock in the morning. Having remained intimate friends, and enjoying each other's society, they probably considered these the pleasantest evenings of their lives. They talked on every subject, especially of what interested and amused Parisians. Their conversation was, as in the majority of salons elsewhere, a verbal rehash of what they had read in the morning papers.

One of the most lively of them was Joseph de Bardon, a celibate living the Parisian life in its fullest and most whimsical manner. He was not a debauche nor depraved, but a singular, happy fellow, still young, for he was scarcely forty. A man of the world in its widest and best sense, gifted with a brilliant, but not profound, mind, with much varied knowledge, but no true erudition, ready comprehension without true understanding, he drew from his observations, his adventures, from everything he saw, met with and found, anecdotes at once comical and philosophical, and made humorous remarks that gave him a great reputation for cleverness in society.

He was the after dinner speaker and had his own story each time, upon which they counted, and he talked without having to be coaxed.

As he sat smoking, his elbows on the table, a petit verre half full beside his plate, half torpid in an atmosphere of tobacco blended with steaming coffee, he seemed to be perfectly at home. He said between two whiffs:

"A curious thing happened to me some time ago."

"Tell it to us," they all exclaimed at once.

"With pleasure. You know that I wander about Paris a great deal, like book collectors who ransack book stalls. I just look at the sights, at the people, at all that is passing by and all that is going on.

"Toward the middle of September—it was beautiful weather—I went out one afternoon, not knowing where I was going. One always has a vague wish to call on some pretty woman or other. One chooses among them in one's mental picture gallery, compares them in one's mind, weighs the interest with which they inspire you, their comparative charms and finally decides according to the influence of the day. But when the sun is very bright and the air warm, it takes away from you all desire to make calls.

"The sun was bright, the air warm. I lighted a cigar and sauntered aimlessly along the outer boulevard. Then, as I strolled on, it occurred to me to walk as far as Montmartre and go into the cemetery.

"I am very fond of cemeteries. They rest me and give me a feeling of sadness; I need it. And, besides, I have good friends in there, those that one no longer goes to call on, and I go there from time to time.

"It is in this cemetery of Montmartre that is buried a romance of my life, a sweetheart who made a great impression on me, a very emotional, charming little woman whose memory, although it causes me great sorrow, also fills me with regrets—regrets of all kinds. And I go to dream beside her grave. She has finished with life.

"And then I like cemeteries because they are immense cities filled to overflowing with inhabitants. Think how many dead people there are in this small space, think of all the generations of Parisians who are housed there forever, veritable troglodytes enclosed in their little vaults, in their little graves covered with a stone or marked by a cross, while living beings take up so much room and make so much noise —imbeciles that they are!

"Then, again, in cemeteries there are monuments almost as interesting as in museums. The tomb of Cavaignac reminded me, I must confess without making any comparison, of the chef d'oeuvre of Jean Goujon: the recumbent statue of Louis de Breze in the subterranean chapel of the Cathedral of Rouen. All modern and realistic art has originated there, messieurs. This dead man, Louis de Breze, is more real, more terrible, more like inanimate flesh still convulsed with the death agony than all the tortured corpses that are distorted to-day in funeral monuments.

"But in Montmartre one can yet admire Baudin's monument, which has a degree of grandeur; that of Gautier, of Murger, on which I saw the other day a simple, paltry wreath of immortelles, yellow immortelles, brought thither by whom? Possibly by the last grisette, very old and now janitress in the neighborhood. It is a pretty little statue by Millet, but ruined by dirt and neglect. Sing of youth, O Murger!

"Well, there I was in Montmartre Cemetery, and was all at once filled with sadness, a sadness that is not all pain, a kind of sadness that makes you think when you are in good health, 'This place is not amusing, but my time has not come yet.'

"The feeling of autumn, of the warm moisture which is redolent of the death of the leaves, and the weakened, weary, anaemic sun increased, while rendering it poetical, the sensation of solitude and of finality that hovered over this spot which savors of human mortality.

"I walked along slowly amid these streets of tombs, where the neighbors do not visit each other, do not sleep together and do not read the newspapers. And I began to read the epitaphs. That is the most amusing thing in the world. Never did Labiche or Meilhac make me laugh as I have laughed at the comical inscriptions on tombstones. Oh, how much superior to the books of Paul de Kock for getting rid of the spleen are these marble slabs and these crosses where the relatives of the deceased have unburdened their sorrow, their desires for the happiness of the vanished ones and their hope of rejoining them—humbugs!

"But I love above all in this cemetery the deserted portion, solitary, full of great yews and cypresses, the older portion, belonging to those dead long since, and which will soon be taken into use again; the growing trees nourished by the human corpses cut down in order to bury in rows beneath little slabs of marble those who have died more recently.

"When I had sauntered about long enough to refresh my mind I felt that I would soon have had enough of it and that I must place the faithful homage of my remembrance on my little friend's last resting place. I felt a tightening of the heart as I reached her grave. Poor dear, she was so dainty, so loving and so white and fresh—and now—if one should open the grave—

"Leaning over the iron grating, I told her of my sorrow in a low tone, which she doubtless did not hear, and was moving away when I saw a woman in black, in deep mourning, kneeling on the next grave. Her crape veil was turned back, uncovering a pretty fair head, the hair in Madonna bands looking like rays of dawn beneath her sombre headdress. I stayed.

"Surely she must be in profound grief. She had covered her face with her hands and, standing there in meditation, rigid as a statue, given up to her grief, telling the sad rosary of her remembrances within the shadow of her concealed and closed eyes, she herself seemed like a dead person mourning another who was dead. All at once a little motion of her back, like a flutter of wind through a willow, led me to suppose that she was going to cry. She wept softly at first, then louder, with quick motions of her neck and shoulders. Suddenly she uncovered her eyes. They were full of tears and charming, the eyes of a bewildered woman, with which she glanced about her as if awaking from a nightmare. She looked at me, seemed abashed and hid her face completely in her hands. Then she sobbed convulsively, and her head slowly bent down toward the marble. She leaned her forehead on it, and her veil spreading around her, covered the white corners of the beloved tomb, like a fresh token of mourning. I heard her sigh, then she sank down with her cheek on the marble slab and remained motionless, unconscious.

"I darted toward her, slapped her hands, blew on her eyelids, while I read this simple epitaph: 'Here lies Louis-Theodore Carrel, Captain of Marine Infantry, killed by the enemy at Tonquin. Pray for him.'

"He had died some months before. I was affected to tears and redoubled my attentions. They were successful. She regained consciousness. I appeared very much moved. I am not bad looking, I am not forty. I saw by her first glance that she would be polite and grateful. She was, and amid more tears she told me her history in detached fragments as well as her gasping breath would allow, how the officer was killed at Tonquin when they had been married a year, how she had married him for love, and being an orphan, she had only the usual dowry.

"I consoled her, I comforted her, raised her and lifted her on her feet. Then I said:

"'Do not stay here. Come.'

"'I am unable to walk,' she murmured.

"'I will support you.'

"'Thank you, sir; you are good. Did you also come to mourn for some one?'

"'Yes, madame.'

"'A dead friend?'

"'Yes, madame.'

"'Your wife?'

"'A friend.'

"'One may love a friend as much as they love their wife. Love has no law.'

"'Yes, madame.'

"And we set off together, she leaning on my arm, while I almost carried her along the paths of the cemetery. When we got outside she faltered:

"'I feel as if I were going to be ill.'

"'Would you like to go in anywhere, to take something?'

"'Yes, monsieur.'

"I perceived a restaurant, one of those places where the mourners of the dead go to celebrate the funeral. We went in. I made her drink a cup of hot tea, which seemed to revive her. A faint smile came to her lips. She began to talk about herself. It was sad, so sad to be always alone in life, alone in one's home, night and day, to have no one on whom one can bestow affection, confidence, intimacy.

"That sounded sincere. It sounded pretty from her mouth. I was touched. She was very young, perhaps twenty. I paid her compliments, which she took in good part. Then, as time was passing, I suggested taking her home in a carriage. She accepted, and in the cab we sat so close that our shoulders touched.

"When the cab stopped at her house she murmured: 'I do not feel equal to going upstairs alone, for I live on the fourth floor. You have been so good. Will you let me take your arm as far as my own door?'

"I agreed with eagerness. She ascended the stairs slowly, breathing hard. Then, as we stood at her door, she said:

"'Come in a few moments so that I may thank you.'

"And, by Jove, I went in. Everything was modest, even rather poor, but simple and in good taste.

"We sat down side by side on a little sofa and she began to talk again about her loneliness. She rang for her maid, in order to offer me some wine. The maid did not come. I was delighted, thinking that this maid probably came in the morning only, what one calls a charwoman.

"She had taken off her hat. She was really pretty, and she gazed at me with her clear eyes, gazed so hard and her eyes were so clear that I was terribly tempted. I caught her in my arms and rained kisses on her eyelids, which she closed suddenly.

"She freed herself and pushed me away, saying:

"'Have done, have done.'

"But I next kissed her on the mouth and she did not resist, and as our glances met after thus outraging the memory of the captain killed in Tonquin, I saw that she had a languid, resigned expression that set my mind at rest.

"I became very attentive and, after chatting for some time, I said:

"'Where do you dine?'

"'In a little restaurant in the neighborhood:
"'All alone?'
"'Why, yes.'
"'Will you dine with me?'
"'Where?'
"'In a good restaurant on the Boulevard.'

"She demurred a little. I insisted. She yielded, saying by way of apology to herself: 'I am so lonely—so lonely.' Then she added:

"'I must put on something less sombre, and went into her bedroom. When she reappeared she was dressed in half-mourning, charming, dainty and slender in a very simple gray dress. She evidently had a costume for the cemetery and one for the town.

"The dinner was very enjoyable. She drank some champagne, brightened up, grew lively and I went home with her.

"This friendship, begun amid the tombs, lasted about three weeks. But one gets tired of everything, especially of women. I left her under pretext of an imperative journey. She made me promise that I would come and see her on my return. She seemed to be really rather attached to me.

"Other things occupied my attention, and it was about a month before I thought much about this little cemetery friend. However, I did not forget her. The recollection of her haunted me like a mystery, like a psychological problem, one of those inexplicable questions whose solution baffles us.

"I do not know why, but one day I thought I might possibly meet her in the Montmartre Cemetery, and I went there.

"I walked about a long time without meeting any but the ordinary visitors to this spot, those who have not yet broken off all relations with their dead. The grave of the captain killed at Tonquin had no mourner on its marble slab, no flowers, no wreath.

"But as I wandered in another direction of this great city of the dead I perceived suddenly, at the end of a narrow avenue of crosses, a couple in deep mourning walking toward me, a man and a woman. Oh, horrors! As they approached I recognized her. It was she!

"She saw me, blushed, and as I brushed past her she gave me a little signal, a tiny little signal with her eye, which meant: 'Do not recognize me!' and also seemed to say, 'Come back to see me again, my dear!'

"The man was a gentleman, distingue, chic, an officer of the Legion of Honor, about fifty years old. He was supporting her as I had supported her myself when we were leaving the cemetery.

"I went my way, filled with amazement, asking myself what this all meant, to what race of beings belonged this huntress of the tombs? Was she just a common girl, one who went to seek among the tombs for men who were in sorrow, haunted by the recollection of some woman, a wife or a sweetheart, and still troubled by the memory of vanished caresses? Was she unique? Are there many such? Is it a profession? Do they parade the cemetery as they parade the street? Or else was she only impressed with the admirable, profoundly philosophical idea of exploiting love recollections, which are revived in these funereal places?

"And I would have liked to know whose widow she was on that special day."

MADEMOISELLE PEARL

I

What a strange idea it was for me to choose Mademoiselle Pearl for queen that evening!

Every year I celebrate Twelfth Night with my old friend Chantal. My father, who was his most intimate friend, used to take me round there when I was a child. I continued the custom, and I doubtless shall continue it as long as I live and as long as there is a Chantal in this world.

The Chantals lead a peculiar existence; they live in Paris as though they were in Grasse, Evetot, or Pont-a-Mousson.

They have a house with a little garden near the observatory. They live there as though they were in the country. Of Paris, the real Paris, they know nothing at all, they suspect nothing; they are so far, so far away! However, from time to time, they take a trip into it. Mademoiselle Chantal goes to lay in her provisions, as it is called in the family. This is how they go to purchase their provisions:

Mademoiselle Pearl, who has the keys to the kitchen closet (for the linen closets are administered by the mistress herself), Mademoiselle Pearl gives warning that the supply of sugar is low, that the preserves are giving out, that there is not much left in the bottom of the coffee bag. Thus warned against famine, Mademoiselle Chantal passes everything in review, taking notes on a pad. Then she puts down a lot of figures and goes through lengthy calculations and long discussions with Mademoiselle Pearl. At last they manage to agree, and they decide upon the quantity of each thing of which they will lay in a three months' provision; sugar, rice, prunes, coffee, preserves, cans of peas, beans, lobster, salt or smoked fish, etc., etc. After which the day for the purchasing is determined on and they go in a cab with a railing round the top and drive to a large grocery store on the other side of the river in the new sections of the town.

Madame Chantal and Mademoiselle Pearl make this trip together, mysteriously, and only return at dinner time, tired out, although still excited, and shaken up by the cab, the roof of which is covered with bundles and bags, like an express wagon.

For the Chantals all that part of Paris situated on the other side of the Seine constitutes the new quarter, a section inhabited by a strange, noisy population, which cares little for honor, spends its days in dissipation, its nights in revelry, and which throws money out of the windows. From time to time, however, the young girls are taken to the Opera-Comique or the Theatre Francais, when the play is recommended by the paper which is read by M. Chantal.

At present the young ladies are respectively nineteen and seventeen. They are two pretty girls, tall and fresh, very well brought up, in fact, too well brought up, so much so that they pass by unperceived like two pretty dolls. Never would the idea come to me to pay the slightest attention or to pay court to one of the young Chantal ladies; they are so immaculate that one hardly dares speak to them; one almost feels indecent when bowing to them.

As for the father, he is a charming man, well educated, frank, cordial, but he likes calm and quiet above all else, and has thus contributed greatly to the mummifying of his family in order to live as he pleased in stagnant quiescence. He reads a lot, loves to talk and is readily affected. Lack of contact and of elbowing with the world has made his moral skin very tender and sensitive. The slightest thing moves him, excites him, and makes him suffer.

The Chantals have limited connections carefully chosen in the neighborhood. They also exchange two or three yearly visits with relatives who live in the distance.

As for me, I take dinner with them on the fifteenth of August and on Twelfth Night. That is as much one of my duties as Easter communion is for a Catholic.

On the fifteenth of August a few friends are invited, but on Twelfth Night I am the only stranger.

Well, this year, as every former year, I went to the Chantals' for my Epiphany dinner.

According to my usual custom, I kissed M. Chantal, Madame Chantal and Mademoiselle Pearl, and I made a deep bow to the Misses Louise and Pauline. I was questioned about a thousand and one things, about what had happened on the boulevards, about politics, about how matters stood in Tong-King, and about our representatives in Parliament. Madame Chantal, a fat lady, whose ideas always gave me the impression of being carved out square like building stones, was accustomed to exclaiming at the end of every political discussion: "All that is seed which does not promise much for the future!" Why have I always imagined that

Madame Chantal's ideas are square? I don't know; but everything that she says takes that shape in my head: a big square, with four symmetrical angles. There are other people whose ideas always strike me as being round and rolling like a hoop. As soon as they begin a sentence on any subject it rolls on and on, coming out in ten, twenty, fifty round ideas, large and small, which I see rolling along, one behind the other, to the end of the horizon. Other people have pointed ideas—but enough of this.

We sat down as usual and finished our dinner without anything out of the ordinary being said. At dessert the Twelfth Night cake was brought on. Now, M. Chantal had been king every year. I don't know whether this was the result of continued chance or a family convention, but he unfailingly found the bean in his piece of cake, and he would proclaim Madame Chantal to be queen. Therefore, I was greatly surprised to find something very hard, which almost made me break a tooth, in a mouthful of cake. Gently I took this thing from my mouth and I saw that it was a little porcelain doll, no bigger than a bean. Surprise caused me to exclaim:

"Ah!" All looked at me, and Chantal clapped his hands and cried: "It's Gaston! It's Gaston! Long live the king! Long live the king!"

All took up the chorus: "Long live the king!" And I blushed to the tip of my ears, as one often does, without any reason at all, in situations which are a little foolish. I sat there looking at my plate, with this absurd little bit of pottery in my fingers, forcing myself to laugh and not knowing what to do or say, when Chantal once more cried out: "Now, you must choose a queen!"

Then I was thunderstruck. In a second a thousand thoughts and suppositions flashed through my mind. Did they expect me to pick out one of the young Chantal ladies? Was that a trick to make me say which one I prefer? Was it a gentle, light, direct hint of the parents toward a possible marriage? The idea of marriage roams continually in houses with grown-up girls, and takes every shape and disguise, and employs every subterfuge. A dread of compromising myself took hold of me as well as an extreme timidity before the obstinately correct and reserved attitude of the Misses Louise and Pauline. To choose one of them in preference to the other seemed to me as difficult as choosing between two drops of water; and then the fear of launching myself into an affair which might, in spite of me, lead me gently into matrimonial ties, by means as wary and imperceptible and as calm as this insignificant royalty—the fear of all this haunted me.

Suddenly I had an inspiration, and I held out to Mademoiselle Pearl the symbolical emblem. At first every one was surprised, then they doubtless appreciated my delicacy and discretion, for they applauded furiously. Everybody was crying: "Long live the queen! Long live the queen!"

As for herself, poor old maid, she was so amazed that she completely lost control of herself; she was trembling and stammering: "No—no—oh! no—not me—please—not me—I beg of you——"

Then for the first time in my life I looked at Mademoiselle Pearl and wondered what she was.

I was accustomed to seeing her in this house, just as one sees old upholstered armchairs on which one has been sitting since childhood without ever noticing them. One day, with no reason at all, because a ray of sunshine happens to strike the seat, you suddenly think: "Why, that chair is very curious"; and then you discover that the wood has been worked by a real artist and that the material is remarkable. I had never taken any notice of Mademoiselle Pearl.

She was a part of the Chantal family, that was all. But how? By what right? She was a tall, thin person who tried to remain in the background, but who was by no means insignificant. She was treated in a friendly manner, better than a housekeeper, not so well as a relative. I suddenly observed several shades of distinction which I had never noticed before. Madame Chantal said: "Pearl." The young ladies: "Mademoiselle Pearl," and Chantal only addressed her as "Mademoiselle," with an air of greater respect, perhaps.

I began to observe her. How old could she be? Forty? Yes, forty. She was not old, she made herself old. I was suddenly struck by this fact. She fixed her hair and dressed in a ridiculous manner, and, notwithstanding all that, she was not in the least ridiculous, she had such simple, natural gracefulness, veiled and hidden. Truly, what a strange creature! How was it I had never observed her before? She dressed her hair in a grotesque manner with little old maid curls, most absurd; but beneath this one could see a large, calm brow, cut by two deep lines, two wrinkles of long sadness, then two blue eyes, large and tender, so timid, so bashful, so humble, two beautiful eyes which had kept the expression of naive wonder of a young girl, of youthful sensations, and also of sorrow, which had softened without spoiling them.

Her whole face was refined and discreet, a face the expression of which seemed to have gone out without being used up or faded by the fatigues and great emotions of life.

What a dainty mouth! and such pretty teeth! But one would have thought that she did not dare smile.

Suddenly I compared her to Madame Chantal! Undoubtedly Mademoiselle Pearl was the better of the two, a hundred times better, daintier, prouder, more noble. I was surprised at my observation. They were pouring out champagne. I held my glass up to the queen and, with a well-turned compliment, I drank to her health. I could see that she felt inclined to hide her head in her napkin. Then, as she was dipping her lips in the clear wine, everybody cried: "The queen drinks! the queen drinks!" She almost turned purple and choked. Everybody was laughing; but I could see that all loved her.

As soon as dinner was over Chantal took me by the arm. It was time for his cigar, a sacred hour. When alone he would smoke it out in the street; when guests came to dinner he would take them to the billiard room and smoke while playing. That evening they had built a fire to celebrate Twelfth Night; my old friend took his cue, a very fine one, and chalked it with great care; then he said:

"You break, my boy!"

He called me "my boy," although I was twenty-five, but he had known me as a young child.

I started the game and made a few carroms. I missed some others, but as the thought of Mademoiselle Pearl kept returning to my mind, I suddenly asked:

"By the way, Monsieur Chantal, is Mademoiselle Pearl a relative of yours?"

Greatly surprised, he stopped playing and looked at me:

"What! Don't you know? Haven't you heard about Mademoiselle Pearl?"

"No."

"Didn't your father ever tell you?"

"No."

"Well, well, that's funny! That certainly is funny! Why, it's a regular romance!"

He paused, and then continued:

"And if you only knew how peculiar it is that you should ask me that to-day, on Twelfth Night!"

"Why?"

"Why? Well, listen. Forty-one years ago to day, the day of the Epiphany, the following events occurred: We were then living at Roily-le-Tors, on the ramparts; but in order that you may understand, I must first explain the house. Roily is built on a hill, or, rather, on a mound which overlooks a great stretch of prairie. We had a house there with a beautiful hanging garden supported by the old battlemented wall; so that the house was in the town on the streets, while the garden overlooked the plain. There was a door leading from the garden to the open country, at the bottom of a secret stairway in the thick wall—the kind you read about in novels. A road passed in front of this door, which was provided with a big bell; for the peasants, in order to avoid the roundabout way, would bring their provisions up this way.

"You now understand the place, don't you? Well, this year, at Epiphany, it had been snowing for a week. One might have thought that the world was coming to an end. When we went to the ramparts to look over the plain, this immense white, frozen country, which shone like varnish, would chill our very souls. One might have thought that the Lord had packed the world in cotton to put it away in the storeroom for old worlds. I can assure you that it was dreary looking.

"We were a very numerous family at that time my father, my mother, my uncle and aunt, my two brothers and four cousins; they were pretty little girls; I married the youngest. Of all that crowd, there are only three of us left: my wife, I, and my sister-in-law, who lives in Marseilles. Zounds! how quickly a family like that dwindles away! I tremble when I think of it! I was fifteen years old then, since I am fifty-six now.

"We were going to celebrate the Epiphany, and we were all happy, very happy! Everybody was in the parlor, awaiting dinner, and my oldest brother, Jacques, said: 'There has been a dog howling out in the plain for about ten minutes; the poor beast must be lost.'

"He had hardly stopped talking when the garden bell began to ring. It had the deep sound of a church bell, which made one think of death. A shiver ran through everybody. My father called the servant and told him to go outside and look. We waited in complete silence; we were thinking of the snow which covered the ground. When the man returned he declared that he had seen nothing. The dog kept up its ceaseless howling, and always from the same spot.

"We sat down to dinner; but we were all uneasy, especially the young people. Everything went well up to the roast, then the bell began to ring again, three times in succession, three heavy, long strokes which vibrated to the tips of our fingers and which stopped our conversation short. We sat there looking at each other, fork in the air, still listening, and shaken by a kind of supernatural fear.

"At last my mother spoke: 'It's surprising that they should have waited so long to come back. Do not go alone, Baptiste; one of these gentlemen will accompany you.'

"My Uncle Francois arose. He was a kind of Hercules, very proud of his strength, and feared nothing in the world. My father said to him: 'Take a gun. There is no telling what it might be.'

"But my uncle only took a cane and went out with the servant.

"We others remained there trembling with fear and apprehension, without eating or speaking. My father tried to reassure us: 'Just wait and see,' he said; 'it will be some beggar or some traveller lost in the snow. After ringing once, seeing that the door was not immediately opened, he attempted again to find his way, and being unable to, he has returned to our door.'

"Our uncle seemed to stay away an hour. At last he came back, furious, swearing: 'Nothing at all; it's some practical joker! There is nothing but that damned dog howling away at about a hundred yards from the walls. If I had taken a gun I would have killed him to make him keep quiet.'

"We sat down to dinner again, but every one was excited; we felt that all was not over, that something was going to happen, that the bell would soon ring again.

"It rang just as the Twelfth Night cake was being cut. All the men jumped up together. My Uncle, Francois, who had been drinking champagne, swore so furiously that he would murder it, whatever it might be, that my mother and my aunt threw themselves on him to prevent his going. My father, although very calm and a little helpless (he limped ever since he had broken his leg when thrown by a horse), declared, in turn, that he wished to find out what was the matter and that he was going. My brothers, aged eighteen and twenty, ran to get their guns; and as no one was paying any attention to me I snatched up a little rifle that was used in the garden and got ready to accompany the expedition.

"It started out immediately. My father and uncle were walking ahead with Baptiste, who was carrying a lantern. My brothers, Jacques and Paul, followed, and I trailed on behind in spite of the prayers of my mother, who stood in front of the house with her sister and my cousins.

"It had been snowing again for the last hour, and the trees were weighted down. The pines were bending under this heavy, white garment, and looked like white pyramids or enormous sugar cones, and through the gray curtains of small hurrying flakes could be seen the lighter bushes which stood out pale in the shadow. The snow was falling so thick that we could hardly see ten feet ahead of us. But the lantern threw a bright light around us. When we began to go down the winding stairway in the wall I really grew frightened. I felt as though some one were walking behind me, were going to grab me by the shoulders and carry me away, and I felt a strong desire to return; but, as I would have had to cross the garden all alone, I did not dare. I heard some one opening the door leading to the plain; my uncle began to swear again, exclaiming: 'By——! He has gone again! If I can catch sight of even his shadow, I'll take care not to miss him, the swine!'

"It was a discouraging thing to see this great expanse of plain, or, rather, to feel it before us, for we could not see it; we could only see a thick, endless veil of snow, above, below, opposite us, to the right, to the left, everywhere. My uncle continued:

"'Listen! There is the dog howling again; I will teach him how I shoot. That will be something gained, anyhow.'

"But my father, who was kind-hearted, went on:

"'It will be much better to go on and get the poor animal, who is crying for hunger. The poor fellow is barking for help; he is calling like a man in distress. Let us go to him.'

"So we started out through this mist, through this thick continuous fall of snow, which filled the air, which moved, floated, fell, and chilled the skin with a burning sensation like a sharp, rapid pain as each flake melted. We were sinking in up to our knees in this soft, cold mass, and we had to lift our feet very high in order to walk. As we advanced the dog's voice became clearer and stronger. My uncle cried: 'Here he is!' We stopped to observe him as one does when he meets an enemy at night.

"I could see nothing, so I ran up to the others, and I caught sight of him; he was frightful and weird-looking; he was a big black shepherd's dog with long hair and a wolf's head, standing just within the gleam of light cast by our lantern on the snow. He did not move; he was silently watching us.

"My uncle said: 'That's peculiar, he is neither advancing nor retreating. I feel like taking a shot at him.'

"My father answered in a firm voice: 'No, we must capture him.'

"Then my brother Jacques added: 'But he is not alone. There is something behind him."

"There was indeed something behind him, something gray, impossible to distinguish. We started out again cautiously. When he saw us approaching the dog sat down. He did not look wicked. Instead, he seemed pleased at having been able to attract the attention of some one.

"My father went straight to him and petted him. The dog licked his hands. We saw that he was tied to the wheel of a little carriage, a sort of toy carriage entirely wrapped up in three or four woolen blankets. We carefully took off these coverings, and as Baptiste approached his lantern to the front of this little vehicle, which looked like a rolling kennel, we saw in it a little baby sleeping peacefully.

"We were so astonished that we couldn't speak.

"My father was the first to collect his wits, and as he had a warm heart and a broad mind, he stretched his hand over the roof of the carriage and said: 'Poor little waif, you shall be one of us!' And he ordered my brother Jacques to roll the foundling ahead of us. Thinking out loud, my father continued:

"'Some child of love whose poor mother rang at my door on this night of Epiphany in memory of the Child of God.'

"He once more stopped and called at the top of his lungs through the night to the four corners of the heavens: 'We have found it!' Then, putting his hand on his brother's shoulder, he murmured: 'What if you had shot the dog, Francois?'

"My uncle did not answer, but in the darkness he crossed himself, for, notwithstanding his blustering manner, he was very religious.

"The dog, which had been untied, was following us.

"Ah! But you should have seen us when we got to the house! At first we had a lot of trouble in getting the carriage up through the winding stairway; but we succeeded and even rolled it into the vestibule.

"How funny mamma was! How happy and astonished! And my four little cousins (the youngest was only six), they looked like four chickens around a nest. At last we took the child from the carriage. It was still sleeping. It was a girl about six weeks old. In its clothes we found ten thousand francs in gold, yes, my boy, ten thousand francs!—which papa saved for her dowry. Therefore, it was not a child of poor people, but, perhaps, the child of some nobleman and a little bourgeoise of the town—or again—we made a thousand suppositions, but we never found out anything-never the slightest clue. The dog himself was recognized by no one. He was a stranger in the country. At any rate, the person who rang three times at our door must have known my parents well, to have chosen them thus.

"That is how, at the age of six weeks, Mademoiselle Pearl entered the Chantal household.

"It was not until later that she was called Mademoiselle Pearl. She was at first baptized 'Marie Simonne Claire,' Claire being intended, for her family name.

"I can assure you that our return to the diningroom was amusing, with this baby now awake and looking round her at these people and these lights with her vague blue questioning eyes.

"We sat down to dinner again and the cake was cut. I was king, and for queen I took Mademoiselle Pearl, just as you did to-day. On that day she did not appreciate the honor that was being shown her.

"Well, the child was adopted and brought up in the family. She grew, and the years flew by. She was so gentle and loving and minded so well that every one would have spoiled her abominably had not my mother prevented it.

"My mother was an orderly woman with a great respect for class distinctions. She consented to treat little Claire as she did her own sons, but, nevertheless, she wished the distance which separated us to be well marked, and our positions well established. Therefore, as soon as the child could understand, she acquainted her with her story and gently, even tenderly, impressed on the little one's mind that, for the Chantals, she was an adopted daughter, taken in, but, nevertheless, a stranger. Claire understood the situation with peculiar intelligence and with surprising instinct; she knew how to take the place which was allotted her, and to keep it with so much tact, gracefulness and gentleness that she often brought tears to my father's eyes. My mother herself was often moved by the passionate gratitude and timid devotion of this dainty and loving little creature that she began calling her: 'My daughter.' At times, when the little one had done something kind and good, my mother would raise her spectacles on her forehead, a thing which always indicated emotion with her, and she would repeat: 'This child is a pearl, a perfect pearl!' This name stuck to the little Claire, who became and remained for us Mademoiselle Pearl."

II

M. Chantal stopped. He was sitting on the edge of the billiard table, his feet hanging, and was playing with a ball with his left hand, while with his right he crumpled a rag which served to rub the chalk marks from the slate. A little red in the face, his voice thick, he was talking away to himself now, lost in his memories, gently drifting through the old scenes and events which awoke in his mind, just as we walk through old family gardens where we were brought up and where each tree, each walk, each hedge reminds us of some occurrence.

I stood opposite him leaning against the wall, my hands resting on my idle cue.

After a slight pause he continued:

"By Jove! She was pretty at eighteen—and graceful—and perfect. Ah! She was so sweet—and good and true—and charming! She had such eyes—blue-transparent—clear—such eyes as I have never seen since!"

He was once more silent. I asked: "Why did she never marry?"

He answered, not to me, but to the word "marry" which had caught his ear: "Why? why? She never would—she never would! She had a dowry of thirty thousand francs, and she received several offers—but she never would! She seemed sad at that time. That was when I married my cousin, little Charlotte, my wife, to whom I had been engaged for six years."

I looked at M. Chantal, and it seemed to me that I was looking into his very soul, and I was suddenly witnessing one of those humble and cruel tragedies of honest, straightforward, blameless hearts, one of those secret tragedies known to no one, not even the silent and resigned victims. A rash curiosity suddenly impelled me to exclaim:

"You should have married her, Monsieur Chantal!"

He started, looked at me, and said:

"I? Marry whom?"

"Mademoiselle Pearl."

"Why?"

"Because you loved her more than your cousin."

He stared at me with strange, round, bewildered eyes and stammered:

"I loved her—I? How? Who told you that?"

"Why, anyone can see that—and it's even on account of her that you delayed for so long your marriage to your cousin who had been waiting for you for six years."

He dropped the ball which he was holding in his left hand, and, seizing the chalk rag in both hands, he buried his face in it and began to sob. He was weeping with his eyes, nose and mouth in a heartbreaking yet ridiculous manner, like a sponge which one squeezes. He was coughing, spitting and blowing his nose in the chalk rag, wiping his eyes and sneezing; then the tears would again begin to flow down the wrinkles on his face and he would make a strange gurgling noise in his throat. I felt bewildered, ashamed; I wanted to run away, and I no longer knew what to say, do, or attempt.

Suddenly Madame Chantal's voice sounded on the stairs. "Haven't you men almost finished smoking your cigars?"

I opened the door and cried: "Yes, madame, we are coming right down."

Then I rushed to her husband, and, seizing him by the shoulders, I cried: "Monsieur Chantal, my friend Chantal, listen to me; your wife is calling; pull yourself together, we must go downstairs."

He stammered: "Yes—yes—I am coming—poor girl! I am coming—tell her that I am coming."

He began conscientiously to wipe his face on the cloth which, for the last two or three years, had been used for marking off the chalk from the slate; then he appeared, half white and half red, his forehead, nose, cheeks and chin covered with chalk, and his eyes swollen, still full of tears.

I caught him by the hands and dragged him into his bedroom, muttering: "I beg your pardon, I beg your pardon, Monsieur Chantal, for having caused you such sorrow—but—I did not know—you—you understand."

He squeezed my hand, saying: "Yes—yes—there are difficult moments."

Then he plunged his face into a bowl of water. When he emerged from it he did not yet seem to me to be presentable; but I thought of a little stratagem. As he was growing worried, looking at himself in the mirror, I said to him: "All you have to do is to say that a little dust flew into your eye and you can cry before everybody to your heart's content."

He went downstairs rubbing his eyes with his handkerchief. All were worried; each one wished to look for the speck, which could not be found; and stories were told of similar cases where it had been necessary to call in a physician.

I went over to Mademoiselle Pearl and watched her, tormented by an ardent curiosity, which was turning to positive suffering. She must indeed have been pretty, with her gentle, calm eyes, so large that it looked as though she never closed them like other mortals. Her gown was a little ridiculous, a real old maid's gown, which was unbecoming without appearing clumsy.

It seemed to me as though I were looking into her soul, just as I had into Monsieur Chantal's; that I was looking right from one end to the other of this humble life, so simple and devoted. I felt an irresistible longing to question her, to find out whether she, too, had loved him; whether she also had suffered, as he had, from this long, secret, poignant grief, which one cannot see, know, or guess, but which breaks forth at night in the loneliness of the dark room. I was watching her, and I could observe her heart beating under her waist, and I wondered whether this sweet, candid face had wept on the soft pillow and she had sobbed, her whole body shaken by the violence of her anguish.

I said to her in a low voice, like a child who is breaking a toy to see what is inside: "If you could have seen Monsieur Chantal crying a while ago it would have moved you."

She started, asking: "What? He was weeping?"

"Ah, yes, he was indeed weeping!"

"Why?"

She seemed deeply moved. I answered:

"On your account."

"On my account?"

"Yes. He was telling me how much he had loved you in the days gone by; and what a pang it had given him to marry his cousin instead of you."

Her pale face seemed to grow a little longer; her calm eyes, which always remained open, suddenly closed so quickly that they seemed shut forever. She slipped from her chair to the floor, and slowly, gently sank down as would a fallen garment.

I cried: "Help! help! Mademoiselle Pearl is ill."

Madame Chantal and her daughters rushed forward, and while they were looking for towels, water and vinegar, I grabbed my hat and ran away.

I walked away with rapid strides, my heart heavy, my mind full of remorse and regret. And yet sometimes I felt pleased; I felt as though I had done a praiseworthy and necessary act. I was asking myself: "Did I do wrong or right?" They had that shut up in their hearts, just as some people carry a bullet in a closed wound. Will they not be happier now? It was too late for their torture to begin over again and early enough for them to remember it with tenderness.

And perhaps some evening next spring, moved by a beam of moonlight falling through the branches on the grass at their feet, they will join and press their hands in memory of all this cruel and suppressed suffering; and, perhaps, also this short embrace may infuse in their veins a little of this thrill which they would not have known without it, and will give to those two dead souls, brought to life in a second, the rapid and divine sensation of this intoxication, of this madness which gives to lovers more happiness in an instant than other men can gather during a whole lifetime!

THE THIEF

While apparently thinking of something else, Dr. Sorbier had been listening quietly to those amazing accounts of burglaries and daring deeds that might have been taken from the trial of Cartouche. "Assuredly," he exclaimed, "assuredly, I know of no viler fault nor any meaner action than to attack a girl's innocence, to corrupt her, to profit by a moment of unconscious weakness and of madness, when her heart is beating like that of a frightened fawn, and her pure lips seek those of her tempter; when she abandons herself without thinking of the irremediable stain, nor of her fall, nor of the morrow.

"The man who has brought this about slowly, viciously, who can tell with what science of evil, and who, in such a case, has not steadiness and self-restraint enough to quench that flame by some icy words, who has not sense enough for two, who cannot recover his self-possession and master the runaway brute within him, and who loses his head on the edge of the precipice over which she is going to fall, is as contemptible as any man who breaks open a lock, or as any rascal on the lookout for a house left defenceless and unprotected or for some easy and dishonest stroke of business, or as that thief whose various exploits you have just related to us.

"I, for my part, utterly refuse to absolve him, even when extenuating circumstances plead in his favor, even when he is carrying on a dangerous flirtation, in which a man tries in vain to keep his balance, not to exceed the limits of the game, any more than at lawn tennis; even when the parts are inverted and a man's adversary is some precocious, curious, seductive girl, who shows you immediately that she has nothing to learn and nothing to experience, except the last chapter of love, one of those girls from whom may fate always preserve our sons, and whom a psychological novel writer has christened 'The Semi-Virgins.'

"It is, of course, difficult and painful for that coarse and unfathomable vanity which is characteristic of every man, and which might be called 'malism', not to stir such a charming fire, difficult to act the Joseph and the fool, to turn away his eyes, and, as it were, to put wax into his ears, like the companions of Ulysses when they were attracted by the divine, seductive songs of the Sirens, difficult only to touch that pretty table covered with a perfectly new cloth, at which you are invited to take a seat before any one else, in such a suggestive voice, and are requested to quench your thirst and to taste that new wine, whose fresh and strange flavor you will never forget. But who would hesitate to exercise such self-restraint if, when he rapidly examines his conscience, in one of those instinctive returns to his sober self in which a man thinks clearly and recovers his head, he were to measure the gravity of his fault, consider it, think of its consequences, of the reprisals, of the uneasiness which he would always feel in the future, and which would destroy the repose and happiness of his life?

"You may guess that behind all these moral reflections, such as a graybeard like myself may indulge in, there is a story hidden, and, sad as it is, I am sure it will interest you on account of the strange heroism it shows."

He was silent for a few moments, as if to classify his recollections, and, with his elbows resting on the arms of his easy-chair and his eyes looking into space, he continued in the slow voice of a hospital professor who is explaining a case to his class of medical students, at a bedside:

"He was one of those men who, as our grandfathers used to say, never met with a cruel woman, the type of the adventurous knight who was always foraging, who had something of the scamp about him, but who despised danger and was bold even to rashness. He was ardent in the pursuit of pleasure, and had an irresistible charm about him, one of those men in whom we excuse the greatest excesses as the most natural things in the world. He had run through all his money at gambling and with pretty girls, and so became, as it were, a soldier of fortune. He amused himself whenever and however he could, and was at that time quartered at Versailles.

"I knew him to the very depths of his childlike heart, which was only too easily seen through and sounded, and I loved him as some old bachelor uncle loves a nephew who plays him tricks, but who knows how to coax him. He had made me his confidant rather than his adviser, kept me informed of his slightest pranks, though he always pretended to be speaking about one of his friends, and not about himself; and I must confess that his youthful impetuosity, his careless gaiety, and his amorous ardor sometimes distracted my thoughts and made me envy the handsome, vigorous young fellow who was so happy at being alive, that I had not the courage to check him, to show him the right road, and to call out to him: 'Take care!' as children do at blind man's buff.

"And one day, after one of those interminable cotillons, where the couples do not leave each other for hours, and can disappear together without anybody thinking of noticing them, the poor fellow at last discovered what love was, that real love which takes up its abode in the very centre of the heart and in the brain, and is proud of being there, and which rules like a sovereign and a tyrannous master, and he became desperately enamored of a pretty but badly brought up girl, who was as disquieting and wayward as she was pretty.

"She loved him, however, or rather she idolized him despotically, madly, with all her enraptured soul and all her being. Left to do as she pleased by imprudent and frivolous parents, suffering from neurosis, in consequence of the unwholesome friendships which she contracted at the convent school, instructed by what she saw and heard and knew was going on around her, in spite of her deceitful and artificial conduct, knowing that neither her father nor her mother, who were very proud of their race as well as avaricious, would ever agree to let her marry the man whom she had taken a liking to, that handsome fellow who had little besides vision, ideas and debts, and who belonged to the middle-class, she laid aside all scruples, thought of nothing but of becoming his, no matter what might be the cost.

"By degrees, the unfortunate man's strength gave way, his heart softened, and he allowed himself to be carried away by that current which buffeted him, surrounded him, and left him on the shore like a waif and a stray.

"They wrote letters full of madness to each other, and not a day passed without their meeting, either accidentally, as it seemed, or at parties and balls. She had yielded her lips to him in long, ardent caresses, which had sealed their compact of mutual passion."

The doctor stopped, and his eyes suddenly filled with tears, as these former troubles came back to his mind; and then, in a hoarse voice, he went on, full of the horror of what he was going to relate:

"For months he scaled the garden wall, and, holding his breath and listening for the slightest noise, like a burglar who is going to break into a house, he went in by the servants' entrance, which she had left open, slunk barefoot down a long passage and up the broad staircase, which creaked occasionally, to the second story, where his sweetheart's room was, and stayed there for hours.

"One night, when it was darker than usual, and he was hurrying lest he should be later than the time agreed on, he knocked up against a piece of furniture in the anteroom and upset it. It so happened that the girl's mother had not gone to sleep, either because she had a sick headache, or else because she had sat up late over some novel, and, frightened at that unusual noise which disturbed the silence of the house, she jumped out of bed, opened the door, saw some one indistinctly running away and keeping close to the wall, and, immediately thinking that there were burglars in the house, she aroused her husband and the servants by her frantic screams. The unfortunate man understood the situation; and, seeing what a terrible fix he was in, and preferring to be taken for a common thief to dishonoring his adored one's name, he ran into the drawing-room, felt on the tables and what-nots, filled his pockets at random with valuable bric-a-brac, and then cowered down behind the grand piano, which barred the corner of a large room.

"The servants, who had run in with lighted candles, found him, and, overwhelming him with abuse, seized him by the collar and dragged him, panting and apparently half dead with shame and terror, to the nearest police station. He defended himself with intentional awkwardness when he was brought up for trial, kept up his part with the most perfect self-possession and without any signs of the despair and anguish that he felt in his heart, and, condemned and degraded and made to suffer martyrdom in his honor as a man and a soldier—he was an officer—he did not protest, but went to prison as one of those criminals whom society gets rid of like noxious vermin.

"He died there of misery and of bitterness of spirit, with the name of the fair-haired idol, for whom he had sacrificed himself, on his lips, as if it had been an ecstatic prayer, and he intrusted his will 'to the priest who administered extreme unction to him, and requested him to give it to me. In it, without mentioning anybody, and without in the least lifting the veil, he at last explained the enigma, and cleared himself of those accusations the terrible burden of which he had borne until his last breath.

"I have always thought myself, though I do not know why, that the girl married and had several charming children, whom she brought up with the austere strictness and in the serious piety of former days!"

CLAIR DE LUNE

Abbe Marignan's martial name suited him well. He was a tall, thin priest, fanatic, excitable, yet upright. All his beliefs were fixed, never varying. He believed sincerely that he knew his God, understood His plans, desires and intentions.

When he walked with long strides along the garden walk of his little country parsonage, he would sometimes ask himself the question: "Why has God done this?" And he would dwell on this continually, putting himself in the place of God, and he almost invariably found an answer. He would never have cried out in an outburst of pious humility: "Thy ways, O Lord, are past finding out."

He said to himself: "I am the servant of God; it is right for me to know the reason of His deeds, or to guess it if I do not know it."

Everything in nature seemed to him to have been created in accordance with an admirable and absolute logic. The "whys" and "becauses" always balanced. Dawn was given to make our awakening pleasant, the days to ripen the harvest, the rains to moisten it, the evenings for preparation for slumber, and the dark nights for sleep.

The four seasons corresponded perfectly to the needs of agriculture, and no suspicion had ever come to the priest of the fact that nature has no intentions; that, on the contrary, everything which exists must conform to the hard demands of seasons, climates and matter.

But he hated woman—hated her unconsciously, and despised her by instinct. He often repeated the words of Christ: "Woman, what have I to do with thee?" and he would add: "It seems as though God, Himself, were dissatisfied with this work of His." She was the tempter who led the first man astray, and who since then had ever been busy with her work of damnation, the feeble creature, dangerous and mysteriously affecting one. And even more than their sinful bodies, he hated their loving hearts.

He had often felt their tenderness directed toward himself, and though he knew that he was invulnerable, he grew angry at this need of love that is always vibrating in them.

According to his belief, God had created woman for the sole purpose of tempting and testing man. One must not approach her without defensive precautions and fear of possible snares. She was, indeed, just like a snare, with her lips open and her arms stretched out to man.

He had no indulgence except for nuns, whom their vows had rendered inoffensive; but he was stern with them, nevertheless, because he felt that at the bottom of their fettered and humble hearts the everlasting tenderness was burning brightly—that tenderness which was shown even to him, a priest.

He felt this cursed tenderness, even in their docility, in the low tones of their voices when speaking to him, in their lowered eyes, and in their resigned tears when he reproved them roughly. And he would shake his cassock on leaving the convent doors, and walk off, lengthening his stride as though flying from danger.

He had a niece who lived with her mother in a little house near him. He was bent upon making a sister of charity of her.

She was a pretty, brainless madcap. When the abbe preached she laughed, and when he was angry with her she would give him a hug, drawing him to her heart, while he sought unconsciously to release himself from this embrace which nevertheless filled him with a sweet pleasure, awakening in his depths the sensation of paternity which slumbers in every man.

Often, when walking by her side, along the country road, he would speak to her of God, of his God. She never listened to him, but looked about her at the sky, the grass and flowers, and one could see the joy of life sparkling in her eyes. Sometimes she would dart forward to catch some flying creature, crying out as she brought it back: "Look, uncle, how pretty it is! I want to hug it!" And this desire to "hug" flies or lilac blossoms disquieted, angered, and roused the priest, who saw, even in this, the ineradicable tenderness that is always budding in women's hearts.

Then there came a day when the sexton's wife, who kept house for Abbe Marignan, told him, with caution, that his niece had a lover.

Almost suffocated by the fearful emotion this news roused in him, he stood there, his face covered with soap, for he was in the act of shaving.

When he had sufficiently recovered to think and speak he cried: "It is not true; you lie, Melanie!"

But the peasant woman put her hand on her heart, saying: "May our Lord judge me if I lie, Monsieur le Cure! I tell you, she goes there every night when your sister has gone to bed. They meet by the river side; you have only to go there and see, between ten o'clock and midnight."

He ceased scraping his chin, and began to walk up and down impetuously, as he always did when he was in deep thought. When he began shaving again he cut himself three times from his nose to his ear.

All day long he was silent, full of anger and indignation. To his priestly hatred of this invincible love was added the exasperation of her spiritual father, of her guardian and pastor, deceived and tricked by a child, and the selfish emotion shown by parents when their daughter announces that she has chosen a husband without them, and in spite of them.

After dinner he tried to read a little, but could not, growing more and, more angry. When ten o'clock struck he seized his cane, a formidable oak stick, which he was accustomed to carry in his nocturnal walks when visiting the sick. And he smiled at the enormous club which he twirled in a threatening manner in his strong, country fist. Then he raised it suddenly and, gritting his teeth, brought it down on a chair, the broken back of which fell over on the floor.

He opened the door to go out, but stopped on the sill, surprised by the splendid moonlight, of such brilliance as is seldom seen.

And, as he was gifted with an emotional nature, one such as had all those poetic dreamers, the Fathers of the Church, he felt suddenly distracted and moved by all the grand and serene beauty of this pale night.

In his little garden, all bathed in soft light, his fruit trees in a row cast on the ground the shadow of their slender branches, scarcely in full leaf, while the giant honeysuckle, clinging to the wall of his house, exhaled a delicious sweetness, filling the warm moonlit atmosphere with a kind of perfumed soul.

He began to take long breaths, drinking in the air as drunkards drink wine, and he walked along slowly, delighted, marveling, almost forgetting his niece.

As soon as he was outside of the garden, he stopped to gaze upon the plain all flooded with the caressing light, bathed in that tender, languishing charm of serene nights. At each moment was heard the short, metallic note of the cricket, and distant nightingales shook out their scattered notes—their light, vibrant music that sets one dreaming, without thinking, a music made for kisses, for the seduction of moonlight.

The abbe walked on again, his heart failing, though he knew not why. He seemed weakened, suddenly exhausted; he wanted to sit down, to rest there, to think, to admire God in His works.

Down yonder, following the undulations of the little river, a great line of poplars wound in and out. A fine mist, a white haze through which the moonbeams passed, silvering it and making it gleam, hung around and above the mountains, covering all the tortuous course of the water with a kind of light and transparent cotton.

The priest stopped once again, his soul filled with a growing and irresistible tenderness.

And a doubt, a vague feeling of disquiet came over him; he was asking one of those questions that he sometimes put to himself.

"Why did God make this? Since the night is destined for sleep, unconsciousness, repose, forgetfulness of everything, why make it more charming than day, softer than dawn or evening? And why does this seductive planet, more poetic than the sun, that seems destined, so discreet is it, to illuminate things too delicate and mysterious for the light of day, make the darkness so transparent?

"Why does not the greatest of feathered songsters sleep like the others? Why does it pour forth its voice in the mysterious night?

"Why this half-veil cast over the world? Why these tremblings of the heart, this emotion of the spirit, this enervation of the body? Why this display of enchantments that human beings do not see, since they are lying in their beds? For whom is destined this sublime spectacle, this abundance of poetry cast from heaven to earth?"

And the abbe could not understand.

But see, out there, on the edge of the meadow, under the arch of trees bathed in a shining mist, two figures are walking side by side.

The man was the taller, and held his arm about his sweetheart's neck and kissed her brow every little while. They imparted life, all at once, to the placid landscape in which they were framed as by a heavenly hand. The two seemed but a single being, the being for whom was destined this calm and silent night, and they came toward the priest as a living answer, the response his Master sent to his questionings.

He stood still, his heart beating, all upset; and it seemed to him that he saw before him some biblical scene, like the loves of Ruth and Boaz, the accomplishment of the will of the Lord, in some of those glorious stories of which the sacred books tell. The verses of the Song of Songs began to ring in his ears, the appeal of passion, all the poetry of this poem replete with tenderness.

And he said unto himself: "Perhaps God has made such nights as these to idealize the love of men."

He shrank back from this couple that still advanced with arms intertwined. Yet it was his niece. But he asked himself now if he would not be disobeying God. And does not God permit love, since He surrounds it with such visible splendor?

And he went back musing, almost ashamed, as if he had intruded into a temple where he had, no right to enter.

WAITER, A "BOCK"

Why did I go into that beer hall on that particular evening? I do not know. It was cold; a fine rain, a flying mist, veiled the gas lamps with a transparent fog, made the side walks reflect the light that streamed from the shop windows—lighting up the soft slush and the muddy feet of the passers-by.

I was going nowhere in particular; was simply having a short walk after dinner. I had passed the Credit Lyonnais, the Rue Vivienne, and several other streets. I suddenly descried a large beer hall which was more than half full. I walked inside, with no object in view. I was not the least thirsty.

I glanced round to find a place that was not too crowded, and went and sat down by the side of a man who seemed to me to be old, and who was smoking a two-sous clay pipe, which was as black as coal. From six to eight glasses piled up on the table in front of him indicated the number of "bocks" he had already absorbed. At a glance I recognized a "regular," one of those frequenters of beer houses who come in the morning when the place opens, and do not leave till evening when it is about to close. He was dirty, bald on top of his head, with a fringe of iron-gray hair falling on the collar of his frock coat. His clothes, much too large for him, appeared to have been made for him at a time when he was corpulent. One could guess that he did not wear suspenders, for he could not take ten steps without having to stop to pull up his trousers. Did he wear a vest? The mere thought of his boots and of that which they covered filled me with horror. The frayed cuffs were perfectly black at the edges, as were his nails.

As soon as I had seated myself beside him, this individual said to me in a quiet tone of voice:

"How goes it?"

I turned sharply round and closely scanned his features, whereupon he continued:

"I see you do not recognize me."

"No, I do not."

"Des Barrets."

I was stupefied. It was Count Jean des Barrets, my old college chum.

I seized him by the hand, and was so dumbfounded that I could find nothing to say. At length I managed to stammer out:

"And you, how goes it with you?"

He responded placidly:

"I get along as I can."

"What are you doing now?" I asked.

"You see what I am doing," he answered quit resignedly.

I felt my face getting red. I insisted:

"But every day?"

"Every day it is the same thing," was his reply, accompanied with a thick puff of tobacco smoke.

He then tapped with a sou on the top of the marble table, to attract the attention of the waiter, and called out:

"Waiter, two 'bocks.'"

A voice in the distance repeated:

"Two bocks for the fourth table."

Another voice, more distant still, shouted out:

"Here they are!"

Immediately a man with a white apron appeared, carrying two "bocks," which he set down, foaming, on the table, spilling some of the yellow liquid on the sandy floor in his haste.

Des Barrets emptied his glass at a single draught and replaced it on the table, while he sucked in the foam that had been left on his mustache. He next asked:

"What is there new?"

I really had nothing new to tell him. I stammered:

"Nothing, old man. I am a business man."

In his monotonous tone of voice he said:

"Indeed, does it amuse you?"

"No, but what can I do? One must do something!"

"Why should one?"

"So as to have occupation."

"What's the use of an occupation? For my part, I do nothing at all, as you see, never anything. When one has not a sou I can understand why one should work. But when one has enough to live on, what's the use? What is the good of working? Do you work for yourself, or for others? If you work for yourself, you do it for your own amusement, which is all right; if you work for others, you are a fool."

Then, laying his pipe on the marble table, he called out anew:

"Waiter, a 'bock.'" And continued: "It makes me thirsty to keep calling so. I am not accustomed to that sort of thing. Yes, yes, I do nothing. I let things slide, and I am growing old. In dying I shall have nothing to regret. My only remembrance will be this beer hall. No wife, no children, no cares, no sorrows, nothing. That is best."

He then emptied the glass which had been brought him, passed his tongue over his lips, and resumed his pipe.

I looked at him in astonishment, and said:

"But you have not always been like that?"

"Pardon me; ever since I left college."

"That is not a proper life to lead, my dear fellow; it is simply horrible. Come, you must have something to do, you must love something, you must have friends."

"No, I get up at noon, I come here, I have my breakfast, I drink my beer, I remain until the evening, I have my dinner, I drink beer. Then about half-past one in the morning, I go home to bed, because the place closes up; that annoys me more than anything. In the last ten years I have passed fully six years on this bench, in my corner; and the other four in my bed, nowhere else. I sometimes chat with the regular customers."

"But when you came to Paris what did you do at first?"

"I paid my devoirs to the Cafe de Medicis."

"What next?"

"Next I crossed the water and came here."

"Why did you take that trouble?"

"What do you mean? One cannot remain all one's life in the Latin Quarter. The students make too much noise. Now I shall not move again. Waiter, a 'bock.'"

I began to think that he was making fun of me, and I continued:

"Come now, be frank. You have been the victim of some great sorrow; some disappointment in love, no doubt! It is easy to see that you are a man who has had some trouble. What age are you?"

"I am thirty, but I look forty-five, at least."

I looked him straight in the face. His wrinkled, ill-shaven face gave one the impression that he was an old man. On the top of his head a few long hairs waved over a skin of doubtful cleanliness. He had enormous eyelashes, a heavy mustache, and a thick beard. Suddenly I had a kind of vision, I know not why, of a basin filled with dirty water in which all that hair had been washed. I said to him:

"You certainly look older than your age. You surely must have experienced some great sorrow."

He replied:

"I tell you that I have not. I am old because I never go out into the air. Nothing makes a man deteriorate more than the life of a cafe."

I still could not believe him.

"You must surely also have been married? One could not get as bald-headed as you are without having been in love."

He shook his head, shaking dandruff down on his coat as he did so.

"No, I have always been virtuous."

And, raising his eyes toward the chandelier which heated our heads, he said:

"If I am bald, it is the fault of the gas. It destroys the hair. Waiter, a 'bock.' Are you not thirsty?"

"No, thank you. But you really interest me. Since when have you been so morbid? Your life is not normal, it is not natural. There is something beneath it all."

"Yes, and it dates from my infancy. I received a great shock when I was very young, and that turned my life into darkness which will last to the end."

"What was it?"

"You wish to know about it? Well, then, listen. You recall, of course, the castle in which I was brought up, for you used to spend five or six months there during vacation. You remember that large gray building, in the middle of a great park, and the long avenues of oaks which opened to the four points of the compass. You remember my father and mother, both of whom were ceremonious, solemn, and severe.

"I worshipped my mother; I was afraid of my father; but I respected both, accustomed always as I was to see every one bow before them. They were Monsieur le Comte and Madame la Comtesse to all the country round, and our neighbors, the Tannemares, the Ravelets, the Brennevilles, showed them the utmost consideration.

"I was then thirteen years old. I was happy, pleased with everything, as one is at that age, full of the joy of life.

"Well, toward the end of September, a few days before returning to college, as I was playing about in the shrubbery of the park, among the branches and leaves, as I was crossing a path, I saw my father and mother, who were walking along.

"I recall it as though it were yesterday. It was a very windy day. The whole line of trees swayed beneath the gusts of wind, groaning, and seeming to utter cries-those dull, deep cries that forests give out during a tempest.

"The falling leaves, turning yellow, flew away like birds, circling and falling, and then running along the path like swift animals.

"Evening came on. It was dark in the thickets. The motion of the wind and of the branches excited me, made me tear about as if I were crazy, and howl in imitation of the wolves.

"As soon as I perceived my parents, I crept furtively toward them, under the branches, in order to surprise them, as though I had been a veritable prowler. But I stopped in fear a few paces from them. My father, who was in a terrible passion, cried:

"'Your mother is a fool; moreover, it is not a question of your mother. It is you. I tell you that I need this money, and I want you to sign this.'

"My mother replied in a firm voice:

"'I will not sign it. It is Jean's fortune. I shall guard it for him and I will not allow you to squander it with strange women, as you have your own heritage.'

"Then my father, trembling with rage, wheeled round and, seizing his wife by the throat, began to slap her with all his might full in the face with his disengaged hand.

"My mother's hat fell off, her hair became loosened and fell over her shoulders; she tried to parry the blows, but she could not do so. And my father, like a madman, kept on striking her. My mother rolled over on the ground, covering her face with her hands. Then he turned her over on her back in order to slap her still more, pulling away her hands, which were covering her face.

"As for me, my friend, it seemed as though the world was coming to an end, that the eternal laws had changed. I experienced the overwhelming dread that one has in presence of things supernatural, in presence of irreparable disasters. My childish mind was bewildered, distracted. I began to cry with all my might, without knowing why; a prey to a fearful dread, sorrow, and astonishment. My father heard me, turned round, and, on seeing me, started toward me. I believe that he wanted to kill me, and I fled like a hunted animal, running straight ahead into the thicket.

"I ran perhaps for an hour, perhaps for two. I know not. Darkness set in. I sank on the grass, exhausted, and lay there dismayed, frantic with fear, and devoured by a sorrow capable of breaking forever the heart of a poor child. I was cold, hungry, perhaps. At length day broke. I was afraid to get up, to walk, to return home, to run farther, fearing to encounter my father, whom I did not wish to see again.

"I should probably have died of misery and of hunger at the foot of a tree if the park guard had not discovered me and led me home by force.

"I found my parents looking as usual. My mother alone spoke to me "'How you frightened me, you naughty boy. I lay awake the whole night.'

"I did not answer, but began to weep. My father did not utter a single word.

"Eight days later I returned to school.

"Well, my friend, it was all over with me. I had witnessed the other side of things, the bad side. I have not been able to perceive the good side since that day. What has taken place in my mind, what strange phenomenon has warped my ideas, I do not know. But I no longer had a taste for anything, a wish for anything, a love for anybody, a desire for anything whatever, any ambition, or any hope. And I always see my poor mother on the ground, in the park, my father beating her. My mother died some years later; my, father still lives. I have not seen him since. Waiter, a 'bock.'"

A waiter brought him his "bock," which he swallowed at a gulp. But, in taking up his pipe again, trembling as he was, he broke it. "Confound it!" he said, with a gesture of annoyance. "That is a real sorrow. It will take me a month to color another!"

And he called out across the vast hall, now reeking with smoke and full of men drinking, his everlasting: "Garcon, un 'bock'— and a new pipe."

AFTER

"My darlings," said the comtesse, "you might go to bed."

The three children, two girls and a boy, rose and kissed their grandmother. Then they said good-night to M. le Cure, who had dined at the chateau, as was his custom every Thursday.

The Abbe Mauduit lifted two of the children on his knees, passing his long arms clad in black round their necks, and kissing them tenderly on the forehead as he drew their heads toward him as a father might.

Then he set them down on the ground, and the little beings went off, the boy ahead, and the girls following.

"You are fond of children, M. le Cure," said the comtesse.

"Very fond, madame."

The old woman raised her bright eyes toward the priest.

"And—has your solitude never weighed too heavily on you?"

"Yes, sometimes."

He became silent, hesitated, and then added: "But I was never made for ordinary life."

"What do you know about it?"

"Oh! I know very well. I was made to be a priest; I followed my vocation."

The comtesse kept staring at him:

"Come now, M. le Cure, tell me this—tell me how it was you resolved to renounce forever all that makes the rest of us love life—all that consoles and sustains us? What is it that drove you, impelled you, to separate yourself from the great natural path of marriage and the family? You are neither an enthusiast nor a fanatic, neither a gloomy person nor a sad person. Was it some incident, some sorrow, that led you to take life vows?"

The Abbe Mauduit rose and approached the fire, then, holding toward the flame his big shoes, such as country priests generally wear, he seemed still hesitating as to what reply he should make.

He was a tall old man with white hair, and for the last twenty years had been pastor of the parish of Saint-Antoine-du-Rocher.

The peasants said of him: "There's a good man for you!" And indeed he was a good man, benevolent, friendly to all, gentle, and, to crown all, generous. Like Saint Martin, he would have cut his cloak in two. He laughed readily, and wept also, on slight provocation, just like a woman—which prejudiced him more or less in the hard minds of the country folk.

The old Comtesse de Saville, living in retirement in her chateau of Rocher, in order to bring up her grandchildren, after the successive deaths of her son and her daughter-in-law, was very much attached to her cure, and used to say of him: "What a heart he has!"

He came every Thursday to spend the evening with the comtesse, and they were close friends, with the frank and honest friendship of old people.

She persisted:

"Look here, M. le Cure! it is your turn now to make a confession!"

He repeated: "I was not made for ordinary life. I saw it fortunately in time, and I have had many proofs since that I made no mistake on the point:

"My parents, who were mercers in Verdiers, and were quite well to do, had great ambitions for me. They sent me to a boarding school while I was very young. No one knows what a boy may suffer at school through the mere fact of separation, of isolation. This monotonous life without affection is good for some, and detestable for others. Young people are often more sensitive than one supposes, and by shutting them up thus too soon, far from those they love, we may develop to an exaggerated extent a sensitiveness which is overwrought and may become sickly and dangerous.

"I scarcely ever played; I had no companions; I passed my hours in homesickness; I spent the whole night weeping in my bed. I sought to bring before my mind recollections of home, trifling memories of little things, little events. I thought incessantly of all I had left behind there. I became almost imperceptibly an over-sensitive youth to whom the slightest annoyances were terrible griefs.

"In this way I remained taciturn, self-absorbed, without expansion, without confidants. This mental excitement was going on secretly and surely. The nerves of children are quickly affected, and one should see to it that they live a tranquil life until they are almost fully developed. But who ever reflects that, for certain boys, an unjust imposition may be as great a pang as the death of a friend in later years? Who can explain why certain young temperaments are liable to terrible emotions for the slightest cause, and may eventually become morbid and incurable?

"This was my case. This faculty of regret developed in me to such an extent that my existence became a martyrdom.

"I did not speak about it; I said nothing about it; but gradually I became so sensitive that my soul resembled an open wound. Everything that affected me gave me painful twitchings, frightful shocks, and consequently impaired my health. Happy are the men whom nature has buttressed with indifference and armed with stoicism.

"I reached my sixteenth year. An excessive timidity had arisen from this abnormal sensitiveness. Feeling myself unprotected from all the attacks of chance or fate, I feared every contact, every approach, every current. I lived as though I were threatened by an unknown and always expected misfortune. I did not venture either to speak or do anything in public. I had, indeed, the feeling that life, is a battle, a dreadful conflict in which one receives terrible blows, grievous, mortal wounds. In place of cherishing, like all men, a cheerful anticipation of the morrow, I had only a confused fear of it, and felt in my own mind a desire to conceal myself to avoid that combat in which I would be vanquished and slain.

"As soon as my studies were finished, they gave me six months' time to choose a career. A very simple occurrence showed me clearly, all of a sudden, the diseased condition of my mind, made me understand the danger, and determined me to flee from it.

"Verdiers is a little town surrounded with plains and woods. In the central street stands my parents' house. I now passed my days far from this dwelling which I had so much regretted, so much desired. Dreams had reawakened in me, and I walked alone in the fields in order to let them escape and fly away. My father and mother, quite occupied with business, and anxious about my future, talked to me only about their profits or about my possible plans. They were fond of me after the manner of hardheaded, practical people; they had more reason than heart in their affection for me. I lived imprisoned in my thoughts, and vibrating with my eternal sensitiveness.

"Now, one evening, after a long walk, as I was making my way home with great strides so as not to be late, I saw a dog trotting toward me. He was a species of red spaniel, very lean, with long curly ears.

"When he was ten paces away from me he stopped. I did the

same. Then he began wagging his tail, and came over to me with short steps and nervous movements of his whole body, bending down on his paws as if appealing to me, and softly shaking his head. I spoke to him. He then began to crawl along in such a sad, humble, suppliant manner that I felt the tears coming into my eyes. I approached him; he ran away, then he came back again; and I bent down on one knee trying to coax him to approach me, with soft words. At last, he was within reach of my hands, and I gently and very carefully stroked him.

"He gained courage, gradually rose and, placing his paws on my shoulders, began to lick my face. He followed me to the house.

"This was really the first being I had passionately loved, because he returned my affection. My attachment to this animal was certainly exaggerated and ridiculous. It seemed to me in a confused sort of way that we were two brothers, lost on this earth, and therefore isolated and without defense, one as well as the other. He never again quitted my side. He slept at the foot of my bed, ate at the table in spite of the objections of my parents, and followed me in my solitary walks.

"I often stopped at the side of a ditch, and sat down in the grass. Sam immediately rushed up, lay down at my feet, and lifted up my hand with his muzzle that I might caress him.

"One day toward the end of June, as we were on the road from Saint-Pierre de Chavrol, I saw the diligence from Pavereau coming along. Its four horses were going at a gallop, with its yellow body, and its imperial with the black leather hood. The coachman cracked his whip; a cloud of dust rose up under the wheels of the heavy vehicle, then floated behind, just as a cloud would do.

"Suddenly, as the vehicle came close to me, Sam, perhaps frightened by the noise and wishing to join me, jumped in front of it. A horse's hoof knocked him down. I saw him roll over, turn round, fall back again beneath the horses' feet, then the coach gave two jolts, and behind it I saw something quivering in the dust on the road. He was nearly cut in two; all his intestines were hanging out and blood was spurting from the wound. He tried to get up, to walk, but he could only move his two front paws, and scratch the ground with them, as if to make a hole. The two others were already dead. And he howled dreadfully, mad with pain.

"He died in a few minutes. I cannot describe how much I felt and suffered. I was confined to my room for a month.

"One night, my father, enraged at seeing me so affected by such a trifling occurrence, exclaimed:

"'How will it be when you have real griefs—if you lose your

wife or children?'

"His words haunted me and I began to see my condition clearly. I understood why all the small miseries of each day assumed in my eyes the importance of a catastrophe; I saw that I was organized in such a way that I suffered dreadfully from everything, that every painful impression was multiplied by my diseased sensibility, and an atrocious fear of life took possession of me. I was without passions, without ambitions; I resolved to sacrifice possible joys in order to avoid sure sorrows. Existence is short, but I made up my mind to spend it in the service of others, in relieving their troubles and enjoying their happiness. Having no direct experience of either one or the other, I should only experience a milder form of emotion.

"And if you only knew how, in spite of this, misery tortures me, ravages me! But what would formerly have been an intolerable affliction has become commiseration, pity.

"These sorrows which cross my path at every moment, I could not endure if they affected me directly. I could not have seen one of my children die without dying myself. And I have, in spite of everything, preserved such a mysterious, overwhelming fear of events that the sight of the postman entering my house makes a shiver pass every day through my veins, and yet I have nothing to be afraid of now."

The Abbe Mauduit ceased speaking. He stared into the fire in the huge grate, as if he saw there mysterious things, all the unknown of the existence he might have passed had he been more fearless in the face of suffering.

He added, then, in a subdued tone:

"I was right. I was not made for this world."

The comtesse said nothing at first; but at length, after a long silence, she remarked:

"For my part, if I had not my grandchildren, I believe I would not have the courage to live."

And the cure rose up without saying another word.

As the servants were asleep in the kitchen, she accompanied him herself to the door, which looked out on the garden, and she saw his tall shadow, lit up by the reflection of the lamp, disappearing through the gloom of night.

Then she came back and sat down before the fire, and pondered over many things we never think of when we are young.

FORGIVENESS

She had been brought up in one of those families who live entirely to themselves, apart from all the rest of the world. Such families know nothing of political events, although they are discussed at table; for changes in the Government take place at such a distance from them that they are spoken of as one speaks of a historical event, such as the death of Louis XVI or the landing of Napoleon.

Customs are modified in course of time, fashions succeed one another, but such variations are taken no account of in the placid family circle where traditional usages prevail year after year. And if some scandalous episode or other occurs in the neighborhood, the disreputable story dies a natural death when it reaches the threshold of the house. The father and mother may, perhaps, exchange a few words on the subject when alone together some evening, but they speak in hushed tones—for even walls have ears. The father says, with bated breath:

"You've heard of that terrible affair in the Rivoil family?"

And the mother answers:

"Who would have dreamed of such a thing? It's dreadful."

The children suspected nothing, and arrive in their turn at years of discretion with eyes and mind blindfolded, ignorant of the real side of life, not knowing that people do not think as they speak, and do not speak as they act; or aware that they should live at war, or at all events, in a state of armed peace, with the rest of mankind; not suspecting the fact that the simple are always deceived, the sincere made sport of, the good maltreated.

Some go on till the day of their death in this blind probity and loyalty and honor, so pure-minded that nothing can open their eyes.

Others, undeceived, but without fully understanding, make mistakes, are dismayed, and become desperate, believing themselves the playthings of a cruel fate, the wretched victims of adverse circumstances, and exceptionally wicked men.

The Savignols married their daughter Bertha at the age of eighteen. She wedded a young Parisian, George Baron by name, who had dealings on the Stock Exchange. He was handsome, well-mannered, and apparently all that could be desired. But in the depths of his heart he somewhat despised his old-fashioned parents-in-law, whom he spoke of among his intimates as "my dear old fossils."

He belonged to a good family, and the girl was rich. They settled down in Paris.

She became one of those provincial Parisians whose name is legion. She remained in complete ignorance of the great city, of its social side, its pleasures and its customs—just as she remained ignorant also of life, its perfidy and its mysteries.

Devoted to her house, she knew scarcely anything beyond her own street; and when she ventured into another part of Paris it seemed to her that she had accomplished a long and arduous journey into some unknown, unexplored city. She would then say to her husband in the evening:

"I have been through the boulevards to-day."

Two or three times a year her husband took her to the theatre. These were events the remembrance of which never grew dim; they provided subjects of conversation for long afterward.

Sometimes three months afterward she would suddenly burst into laughter, and exclaim:

"Do you remember that actor dressed up as a general, who crowed like a cock?"

Her friends were limited to two families related to her own. She spoke of them as "the Martinets" and "the Michelins."

Her husband lived as he pleased, coming home when it suited him —sometimes not until dawn—alleging business, but not putting himself out overmuch to account for his movements, well aware that no suspicion would ever enter his wife's guileless soul.

But one morning she received an anonymous letter.

She was thunderstruck—too simple-minded to understand the infamy of unsigned information and to despise the letter, the writer of which declared himself inspired by interest in her happiness, hatred of evil, and love of truth.

This missive told her that her husband had had for two years past, a sweetheart, a young widow named Madame Rosset, with whom he spent all his evenings.

Bertha knew neither how to dissemble her grief nor how to spy on her husband. When he came in for lunch she threw the letter down before him, burst into tears, and fled to her room.

He had time to take in the situation and to prepare his reply. He knocked at his wife's door. She opened it at once, but dared not look at him. He smiled, sat down, drew her to his knee, and in a tone of light raillery began:

"My dear child, as a matter of fact, I have a friend named Madame Rosset, whom I have known for the last ten years, and of whom I have a very high opinion. I may add that I know scores of other people whose names I have never mentioned to you, seeing that you do not care for society, or fresh acquaintances, or functions of any sort. But, to make short work of such vile accusations as this, I want you to put on your things after lunch, and we'll go together and call on this lady, who will very soon become a friend of yours, too, I am quite sure."

She embraced her husband warmly, and, moved by that feminine spirit of curiosity which will not be lulled once it is aroused, consented to go and see this unknown widow, of whom she was, in spite of everything, just the least bit jealous. She felt instinctively that to know a danger is to be already armed against it.

She entered a small, tastefully furnished flat on the fourth floor of an attractive house. After waiting five minutes in a drawing-room rendered somewhat dark by its many curtains and hangings, a door opened, and a very dark, short, rather plump young woman appeared, surprised and smiling.

George introduced them:

"My wife—Madame Julie Rosset."

The young widow uttered a half-suppressed cry of astonishment and joy, and ran forward with hands outstretched. She had not hoped, she said, to have this pleasure, knowing that Madame Baron never saw any one, but she was delighted to make her acquaintance. She was so fond of George (she said "George" in a familiar, sisterly sort of way) that, she had been most anxious to know his young wife and to make friends with her, too.

By the end of a month the two new friends were inseparable. They saw each other every day, sometimes twice a day, and dined together every evening, sometimes at one house, sometimes at the other. George no longer deserted his home, no longer talked of pressing business. He adored his own fireside, he said.

When, after a time, a flat in the house where Madame Rosset lived became vacant Madame Baron hastened to take it, in order to be near her friend and spend even more time with her than hitherto.

And for two whole years their friendship was without a cloud, a friendship of heart and mind—absolute, tender, devoted. Bertha could hardly speak without bringing in Julie's name. To her Madame Rosset represented perfection.

She was utterly happy, calm and contented.

But Madame Rosset fell ill. Bertha hardly left her side. She spent her nights with her, distracted with grief; even her husband seemed inconsolable.

One morning the doctor, after leaving the invalid's bedside, took George and his wife aside, and told them that he considered Julie's condition very grave.

As soon as he had gone the grief-stricken husband and wife sat down opposite each other and gave way to tears. That night they both sat up with the patient. Bertha tenderly kissed her friend from time to time, while George stood at the foot of the bed, his eyes gazing steadfastly on the invalid's face.

The next day she was worse.

But toward evening she declared she felt better, and insisted that her friends should go back to their own apartment to dinner.

They were sitting sadly in the dining-room, scarcely even attempting to eat, when the maid gave George a note. He opened it, turned pale as death, and, rising from the table, said to his wife in a constrained voice:

"Wait for me. I must leave you a moment. I shall be back in ten minutes. Don't go away on any account."

And he hurried to his room to get his hat.

Bertha waited for him, a prey to fresh anxiety. But, docile in everything, she would not go back to her friend till he returned.

At length, as he did not reappear, it occurred to her to visit his room and see if he had taken his gloves. This would show whether or not he had had a call to make.

She saw them at the first glance. Beside them lay a crumpled paper, evidently thrown down in haste.

She recognized it at once as the note George had received.

And a burning temptation, the first that had ever assailed her urged her to read it and discover the cause of her husband's abrupt departure. Her rebellious conscience protested but a devouring and fearful curiosity prevailed. She seized the paper, smoothed it out, recognized the tremulous, penciled writing as Julie's, and read:

"Come alone and kiss me, my poor dear. I am dying."

At first she did not understand, the idea of Julie's death being her uppermost thought. But all at once the true meaning of what she read burst in a flash upon her; this penciled note threw a lurid light upon her whole existence, revealed the whole infamous truth, all the treachery and perfidy of which she had been the victim. She understood the long years of deceit, the way in which she had been made their puppet. She saw them again, sitting side by side in the evening, reading by lamplight out of the same book, glancing at each other at the end of each page.

And her poor, indignant, suffering, bleeding heart was cast into the depths of a despair which knew no bounds.

Footsteps drew near; she fled, and shut herself in her own room. Presently her husband called her:

"Come quickly! Madame Rosset is dying."

Bertha appeared at her door, and with trembling lips replied:

"Go back to her alone; she does not need me."

He looked at her stupidly, dazed with grief, and repeated:

"Come at once! She's dying, I tell you!"

Bertha answered:

"You would rather it were I."

Then at last he understood, and returned alone to the dying woman's bedside.

He mourned her openly, shamelessly, indifferent to the sorrow of the wife who no longer spoke to him, no longer looked at him; who passed her life in solitude, hedged round with disgust, with indignant anger, and praying night and day to God.

They still lived in the same house, however, and sat opposite each other at table, in silence and despair.

Gradually his sorrow grew less acute; but she did not forgive him.

And so their life went on, hard and bitter for them both.

For a whole year they remained as complete strangers to each other as if they had never met. Bertha nearly lost her reason.

At last one morning she went out very early, and returned about eight o'clock bearing in her hands an enormous bouquet of white roses. And she sent word to her husband that she wanted to speak to him. He came-anxious and uneasy.

"We are going out together," she said. "Please carry these flowers; they are too heavy for me."

A carriage took them to the gate of the cemetery, where they alighted. Then, her eyes filling with tears, she said to George:

"Take me to her grave."

He trembled, and could not understand her motive; but he led the way, still carrying the flowers. At last he stopped before a white marble slab, to which he pointed without a word.

She took the bouquet from him, and, kneeling down, placed it on the grave. Then she offered up a silent, heartfelt prayer.

Behind her stood her husband, overcome by recollections of the past.

She rose, and held out her hands to him.

"If you wish it, we will be friends," she said.

IN THE SPRING

With the first day of spring, when the awakening earth puts on its garment of green, and the warm, fragrant air fans our faces and fills our lungs and appears even to penetrate to our hearts, we experience a vague, undefined longing for freedom, for happiness, a desire to run, to wander aimlessly, to breathe in the spring. The previous winter having been unusually severe, this spring feeling was like a form of intoxication in May, as if there were an overabundant supply of sap.

One morning on waking I saw from my window the blue sky glowing in the sun above the neighboring houses. The canaries hanging in the windows were singing loudly, and so were the servants on every floor; a cheerful noise rose up from the streets, and I went out, my spirits as bright as the day, to go—I did not exactly know where. Everybody I met seemed to be smiling; an air of happiness appeared to pervade everything in the warm light of returning spring. One might almost have said that a breeze of love was blowing through the city, and the sight of the young women whom I saw in the streets in their morning toilets, in the depths of whose eyes there lurked a hidden tenderness, and who walked with languid grace, filled my heart with agitation.

Without knowing how or why, I found myself on the banks of the Seine. Steamboats were starting for Suresnes, and suddenly I was seized by an unconquerable desire to take a walk through the woods. The deck of the Mouche was covered with passengers, for the sun in early spring draws one out of the house, in spite of themselves, and everybody moves about, goes and comes and talks to his neighbor.

I had a girl neighbor; a little work-girl, no doubt, who possessed the true Parisian charm: a little head, with light curly hair, which looked like a shimmer of light as it danced in the wind, came down to her ears, and descended to the nape of her neck, where it became such fine, light-colored clown that one could scarcely see it, but felt an irresistible desire to shower kisses on it.

Under my persistent gaze, she turned her head toward me, and then immediately looked down, while a slight crease at the side of her mouth, that was ready to break out into a smile, also showed a fine, silky, pale down which the sun was gilding a little.

The calm river grew wider; the atmosphere was warm and perfectly still, but a murmur of life seemed to fill all space.

My neighbor raised her eyes again, and this time, as I was still looking at her, she smiled decidedly. She was charming, and in her passing glance I saw a thousand things, which I had hitherto been ignorant of, for I perceived unknown depths, all the charm of tenderness, all the poetry which we dream of, all the happiness which we are continually in search of. I felt an insane longing to open my arms and to carry her off somewhere, so as to whisper the sweet music of words of love into her ears.

I was just about to address her when somebody touched me on the shoulder, and as I turned round in some surprise, I saw an ordinary-looking man, who was neither young nor old, and who gazed at me sadly.

"I should like to speak to you," he said.

I made a grimace, which he no doubt saw, for he added:

"It is a matter of importance."

I got up, therefore, and followed him to the other end of the boat and then he said:

"Monsieur, when winter comes, with its cold, wet and snowy weather, your doctor says to you constantly: 'Keep your feet warm, guard against chills, colds, bronchitis, rheumatism and pleurisy.'

"Then you are very careful, you wear flannel, a heavy greatcoat and thick shoes, but all this does not prevent you from passing two months in bed. But when spring returns, with its leaves and flowers, its warm, soft breezes and its smell of the fields, all of which causes you vague disquiet and causeless emotion, nobody says to you:

"'Monsieur, beware of love! It is lying in ambush everywhere; it is watching for you at every corner; all its snares are laid, all its weapons are sharpened, all its guiles are prepared! Beware of love! Beware of love! It is more dangerous than brandy, bronchitis or pleurisy! It never forgives and makes everybody commit irreparable follies.'

"Yes, monsieur, I say that the French Government ought to put large public notices on the walls, with these words: 'Return of spring. French citizens, beware of love!' just as they put: 'Beware of paint:

"However, as the government will not do this, I must supply its place, and I say to you: 'Beware of love!' for it is just going to seize you, and it is my duty to inform you of it, just as in Russia they inform any one that his nose is frozen."

I was much astonished at this individual, and assuming a dignified manner, I said:

"Really, monsieur, you appear to me to be interfering in a matter which is no concern of yours."

He made an abrupt movement and replied:

"Ah! monsieur, monsieur! If I see that a man is in danger of being drowned at a dangerous spot, ought I to let him perish? So just listen to my story and you will see why I ventured to speak to you like this.

"It was about this time last year that it occurred. But, first of all, I must tell you that I am a clerk in the Admiralty, where our chiefs, the commissioners, take their gold lace as quill-driving officials seriously, and treat us like forecastle men on board a ship. Well, from my office I could see a small bit of blue sky and the swallows, and I felt inclined to dance among my portfolios.

"My yearning for freedom grew so intense that, in spite of my repugnance, I went to see my chief, a short, bad-tempered man, who was always in a rage. When I told him that I was not well, he looked at me and said: 'I do not believe it, monsieur, but be off with you! Do you think that any office can go on with clerks like you?' I started at once and went down the Seine. It was a day like this, and I took the Mouche, to go as far as Saint Cloud. Ah! what a good thing it would have been if my chief had refused me permission to leave the office that day!

"I seemed to myself to expand in the sun. I loved everything—the steamer, the river, the trees, the houses and my fellow-passengers. I felt inclined to kiss something, no matter what; it was love, laying its snare. Presently, at the Trocadero, a girl, with a small parcel in her hand, came on board and sat down opposite me. She was decidedly pretty, but it is surprising, monsieur, how much prettier women seem to us when the day is fine at the beginning of the spring. Then they have an intoxicating charm, something quite peculiar about them. It is just like drinking wine after cheese.

"I looked at her and she also looked at me, but only occasionally, as that girl did at you, just now; but at last, by dint of looking at each other constantly, it seemed to me that we knew each other well enough to enter into conversation, and I spoke to her and she replied. She was decidedly pretty and nice and she intoxicated me, monsieur!

"She got out at Saint-Cloud, and I followed her. She went and delivered her parcel, and when she returned the boat had just started. I walked by her side, and the warmth of the air made us both sigh. 'It would be very nice in the woods,' I said. 'Indeed, it would!' she replied. 'Shall we go there for a walk, mademoiselle?'

"She gave me a quick upward look, as if to see exactly what I was like, and then, after a little hesitation, she accepted my proposal, and soon we were there, walking side by side. Under the foliage, which was still rather scanty, the tall, thick, bright green grass was inundated by the sun, and the air was full of insects that were also making love to one another, and birds were singing in all directions. My companion began to jump and to run, intoxicated by the air and the smell of the country, and I ran and jumped, following her example. How silly we are at times, monsieur!

"Then she sang unrestrainedly a thousand things, opera airs and the song of Musette! The song of Musette! How poetical it seemed to me, then! I almost cried over it. Ah! Those silly songs make us lose our heads; and, believe me, never marry a woman who sings in the country, especially if she sings the song of Musette!

"She soon grew tired, and sat down on a grassy slope, and I sat at her feet and took her hands, her little hands, that were so marked with the needle, and that filled me with emotion. I said to myself:

"'These are the sacred marks of toil.' Oh! monsieur, do you know what those sacred marks of toil mean? They mean all the gossip of the workroom, the whispered scandal, the mind soiled by all the filth that is talked; they mean lost chastity, foolish chatter, all the wretchedness of their everyday life, all the narrowness of ideas which belongs to women of the lower orders, combined to their fullest extent in the girl whose fingers bear the sacred marks of toil.

"Then we looked into each other's eyes for a long while. Oh! what power a woman's eye has! How it agitates us, how it invades our very being, takes possession of us, and dominates us! How profound it seems, how full of infinite promises! People call that looking into each other's souls! Oh! monsieur, what humbug! If we could see into each other's souls, we should be more careful of what we did. However, I was captivated and was crazy about her and tried to take her into my arms, but she said: 'Paws off!'. Then I knelt down and opened my heart to her and poured out all the affection that was suffocating me. She seemed surprised at my change of manner and gave me a sidelong glance, as if to say, 'Ah! so that is the way women make a fool of you, old fellow! Very well, we will see.'

"In love, monsieur, we are always novices, and women artful dealers.

"No doubt I could have had her, and I saw my own stupidity later, but what I wanted was not a woman's person, it was love, it was the ideal. I was sentimental, when I ought to have been using my time to a better purpose.

"As soon as she had had enough of my declarations of affection, she got up, and we returned to Saint-Cloud, and I did not leave her until we got to Paris; but she had looked so sad as we were returning, that at last I asked her what was the matter. 'I am thinking,' she replied, 'that this has been one of those days of which we have but few in life.' My heart beat so that it felt as if it would break my ribs.

"I saw her on the following Sunday, and the next Sunday, and every Sunday. I took her to Bougival, Saint-Germain, Maisons-Lafitte, Poissy; to every suburban resort of lovers.

"The little jade, in turn, pretended to love me, until, at last, I altogether lost my head, and three months later I married her.

"What can you expect, monsieur, when a man is a clerk, living alone, without any relations, or any one to advise him? One says to one's self: 'How sweet life would be with a wife!'

"And so one gets married and she calls you names from morning till night, understands nothing, knows nothing, chatters continually, sings the song of Musette at the, top of her voice (oh! that song of Musette, how tired one gets of it!); quarrels with the charcoal dealer, tells the janitor all her domestic details, confides all the secrets of her bedroom to the neighbor's servant, discusses her husband with the tradespeople and has her head so stuffed with stupid stories, with idiotic superstitions, with extraordinary ideas and monstrous prejudices, that I—for what I have said applies more particularly to myself—shed tears of discouragement every time I talk to her."

He stopped, as he was rather out of breath and very much moved, and I looked at him, for I felt pity for this poor, artless devil, and I was just going to give him some sort of answer, when the boat stopped. We were at Saint-Cloud.

The little woman who had so taken my fancy rose from her seat in order to land. She passed close to me, and gave me a sidelong glance and a furtive smile, one of those smiles that drive you wild. Then she jumped on the landing-stage. I sprang forward to follow her, but my neighbor laid hold of my arm. I shook myself loose, however, whereupon he seized the skirt of my coat and pulled me back, exclaiming: "You shall not go! you shall not go!" in such a loud voice that everybody turned round and laughed, and I remained standing motionless and furious, but without venturing to face scandal and ridicule, and the steamboat started.

The little woman on the landing-stage looked at me as I went off with an air of disappointment, while my persecutor rubbed his hands and whispered to me:

"You must acknowledge that I have done you a great service."

A QUEER NIGHT IN PARIS

*M*attre Saval, notary at Vernon, was passionately fond of music. Although still young he was already bald; he was always carefully shaven, was somewhat corpulent as was suitable, and wore a gold pince-nez instead of spectacles. He was active, gallant and cheerful and was considered quite an artist in Vernon. He played the piano and the violin, and gave musicals where the new operas were interpreted.

He had even what is called a bit of a voice; nothing but a bit, very little bit of a voice; but he managed it with so much taste that cries of "Bravo!" "Exquisite!" "Surprising!" "Adorable!" issued from every throat as soon as he had murmured the last note.

He subscribed to a music publishing house in Paris, and they sent him the latest music, and from time to time he sent invitations after this fashion to the elite of the town:

"You are invited to be present on Monday evening at the house of M. Saval, notary, Vernon, at the first rendering of 'Sais.'"

A few officers, gifted with good voices, formed the chorus. Two or three lady amateurs also sang. The notary filled the part of leader of the orchestra with so much correctness that the bandmaster of the 190th regiment of the line said of him, one day, at the Cafe de l'Europe.

"Oh! M. Saval is a master. It is a great pity that he did not adopt the career of an artist."

When his name was mentioned in a drawing-room, there was always somebody found to declare: "He is not an amateur; he is an artist, a genuine artist."

And two or three persons repeated, in a tone of profound conviction:

"Oh! yes, a genuine artist," laying particular stress on the word "genuine."

Every time that a new work was interpreted at a big Parisian theatre M. Saval paid a visit to the capital.

Now, last year, according to his custom, he went to hear Henri VIII. He then took the express which arrives in Paris at 4:30 P.M., intending to return by the 12:35 A.M. train, so as not to have to sleep at a hotel. He had put on evening dress, a black coat and white tie, which he concealed under his overcoat with the collar turned up.

As soon as he set foot on the Rue d'Amsterdam, he felt himself in quite jovial mood. He said to himself:

"Decidedly, the air of Paris does not resemble any other air. It has in it something indescribably stimulating, exciting, intoxicating, which fills you with a strange longing to dance about and to do many other things. As soon as I arrive here, it seems to me, all of a sudden, that I have taken a bottle of champagne. What a life one can lead in this city in the midst of artists! Happy are the elect, the great men who make themselves a reputation in such a city! What an existence is theirs!"

And he made plans; he would have liked to know some of these celebrated men, to talk about them in Vernon, and to spend an evening with them from time to time in Paris.

But suddenly an idea struck him. He had heard allusions to little cafes in the outer boulevards at which well-known painters, men of letters, and even musicians gathered, and he proceeded to go up to Montmartre at a slow pace.

He had two hours before him. He wanted to look about him. He passed in front of taverns frequented by belated bohemians, gazing at the different faces, seeking to discover the artists. Finally, he came to the sign of "The Dead Rat," and, allured by the name, he entered.

Five or six women, with their elbows resting on the marble tables, were talking in low tones about their love affairs, the quarrels of Lucie and Hortense, and the scoundrelism of Octave. They were no longer young, were too fat or too thin, tired out, used up. You could see that they were almost bald; and they drank beer like men.

M. Saval sat down at some distance from them and waited, for the hour for taking absinthe was at hand.

A tall young man soon came in and took a seat beside him. The landlady called him M. "Romantin." The notary quivered. Was this the Romantin who had taken a medal at the last Salon?

The young man made a sign to the waiter.

"You will bring up my dinner at once, and then carry to my new studio, 15 Boulevard de Clichy, thirty bottles of beer, and the ham I ordered this morning. We are going to have a housewarming."

M. Saval immediately ordered dinner. Then, he took off his overcoat, so that his dress suit and his white tie could be seen. His neighbor did not seem to notice him. He had taken up a newspaper, and was reading it. M. Saval glanced sideways at him, burning with the desire to speak to him.

Two young men entered, in red vests and with peaked beards, in the fashion of Henry III. They sat down opposite Romantin.

The first of the pair said:

"Is it for this evening?"

Romantin pressed his hand.

"I believe you, old chap, and everyone will be there. I have Bonnat, Guillemet, Gervex, Beraud, Hebert, Duez, Clairin, and Jean-Paul Laurens. It will be a stunning affair! And women, too! Wait till you see! Every actress without exception—of course I mean, you know, all those who have nothing to do this evening."

The landlord of the establishment came across.

"Do you often have this housewarming?"

The painter replied:

"I believe you, every three months, each quarter."

M. Saval could not restrain himself any longer, and in a hesitating voice said:

"I beg your pardon for intruding on you, monsieur, but I heard your name mentioned, and I would be very glad to know if you really are M. Romantin, whose work in the last Salon I have so much admired?"

The painter answered:

"I am the very person, monsieur."

The notary then paid the artist a very well-turned compliment, showing that he was a man of culture.

The painter, gratified, thanked him politely in reply.

Then they chattered. Romantin returned to the subject of his house-warming, going into details as to the magnificence of the forthcoming entertainment.

M. Saval questioned him as to all the men he was going to receive, adding:

"It would be an extraordinary piece of good fortune for a stranger to meet at one time so many celebrities assembled in the studio of an artist of your rank."

Romantin, vanquished, replied:

"If it would be agreeable to you, come."

M. Saval accepted the invitation with enthusiasm, reflecting:

"I shall have time enough to see Henri VIII."

Both of them had finished their meal. The notary insisted on paying the two bills, wishing to repay his neighbor's civilities. He also paid for the drinks of the young fellows in red velvet; then he left the establishment with the painter.

They stopped in front of a very long, low house, the first story having the appearance of an interminable conservatory. Six studios stood in a row with their fronts facing the boulevards.

Romantin was the first to enter, and, ascending the stairs, he opened a door, and lighted a match and then a candle.

They found themselves in an immense apartment, the furniture of which consisted of three chairs, two easels, and a few sketches standing on the ground along the walls. M. Saval remained standing at the door somewhat astonished.

The painter remarked:

"Here you are! we've got to the spot; but everything has yet to be done."

Then, examining the high, bare apartment, its ceiling disappearing in the darkness, he said:

"We might make a great deal out of this studio."

He walked round it, surveying it with the utmost attention, then went on:

"I know someone who might easily give a helping hand. Women are incomparable for hanging drapery. But I sent her to the country for to-day in order to get her off my hands this evening. It is not that she bores me, but she is too much lacking in the ways of good society. It would be embarrassing to my guests."

He reflected for a few seconds, and then added:

"She is a good girl, but not easy to deal with. If she knew that I was holding a reception, she would tear out my eyes."

M. Saval had not even moved; he did not understand.

The artist came over to him.

"Since I have invited you, you will assist me about something."

The notary said emphatically:

"Make any use of me you please. I am at your disposal."

Romantin took off his jacket.

"Well, citizen, to work!' We are first going to clean up."

He went to the back of the easel, on which there was a canvas representing a cat, and seized a very worn-out broom.

"I say! Just brush up while I look after the lighting."

M. Saval took the broom, inspected it, and then began to sweep the floor very awkwardly, raising a whirlwind of dust.

Romantin, disgusted, stopped him: "Deuce take it! you don't know how to sweep the floor! Look at me!"

And he began to roll before him a heap of grayish sweepings, as if he had done nothing else all his life. Then, he gave bark the broom to the notary, who imitated him.

In five minutes, such a cloud of dust filled the studio that Rormantin asked:

"Where are you? I can't see you any longer."

M. Saval, who was coughing, came near to him. The painter said:

"How would you set about making a chandelier?"

The other, surprised, asked:

"What chandelier?"

"Why, a chandelier to light the room—a chandelier with wax-candles."

The notary did not understand.

He answered: "I don't know."

The painter began to jump about, cracking his fingers.

"Well, monseigneur, I have found out a way."

Then he went on more calmly:

"Have you got five francs about you?"

M. Saval replied:

"Why, yes."

The artist said: "Well! you'll go out and buy for me five francs' worth of wax-candles while I go and see the cooper."

And he pushed the notary in his evening coat into the street. At the end of five minutes, they had returned, one of them with the wax-candles and the other with the hoop of a cask. Then Romantin plunged his hand into a cupboard, and drew forth twenty empty bottles, which he fixed in the form of a crown around the hoop.

He then went downstairs to borrow a ladder from the janitress, after having explained that he had made interest with the old woman by painting the portrait of her cat, exhibited on the easel.

When he returned with the ladder, he said to M. Saval:

"Are you active?"

The other, without understanding, answered:

"Why, yes."

"Well, you just climb up there, and fasten this chandelier for me to the ring of the ceiling. Then, you put a wax-candle in each bottle, and light it. I tell you I have a genius for lighting up. But off with your coat, damn it! You are just like a Jeames."

The door was opened brusquely. A woman appeared, her eyes flashing, and remained standing on the threshold.

Romantin gazed at her with a look of terror.

She waited some seconds, crossing her arms over her breast, and then in a shrill, vibrating, exasperated voice said:

"Ha! you dirty scoundrel, is this the way you leave me?"

Romantin made no reply. She went on:

"Ha! you scoundrel! You did a nice thing in parking me off to the country. You'll soon see the way I'll settle your jollification. Yes, I'm going to receive your friends."

She grew warmer.

"I'm going to slap their faces with the bottles and the wax-candles——"

Romantin said in a soft tone:

"Mathilde——"

But she did not pay any attention to him; she went on:

"Wait a little, my fine fellow! wait a little!"

Romantin went over to her, and tried to take her by the hands.

"Mathilde——"

But she was now fairly under way; and on she went, emptying the vials of her wrath with strong words and reproaches. They flowed out of her mouth like, a stream sweeping a heap of filth along with it. The words pouring forth seemed struggling for exit. She stuttered, stammered, yelled, suddenly recovering her voice to cast forth an insult or a curse.

He seized her hands without her having noticed it. She did not seem to see anything, so taken up was she in scolding and relieving her feelings. And suddenly she began to weep. The tears flowed from her eyes, but this did not stop her complaints. But her words were uttered in a screaming falsetto voice with tears in it and interrupted by sobs. She commenced afresh twice or three times, till she stopped as if something were choking her, and at last she ceased with a regular flood of tears.

Then he clasped her in his arms and kissed her hair, affected himself.

"Mathilde, my little Mathilde, listen. You must be reasonable. You know, if I give a supper-party to my friends, it is to thank these gentlemen for the medal I got at the Salon. I cannot receive women. You ought to understand that. It is not the same with artists as with other people."

She stammered, in the midst of her tears:

"Why didn't you tell me this?"

He replied:

"It was in order not to annoy you, not to give you pain. Listen, I'm going to see you home. You will be very sensible, very nice; you will remain quietly waiting for me in bed, and I'll come back as soon as it's over."

She murmured:

"Yes, but you will not begin over again?"

"No, I swear to you!"

He turned towards M. Saval, who had at last hooked on the chandelier:

"My dear friend, I am coming back in five minutes. If anyone arrives in my absence, do the honors for me, will you not?"

And he carried off Mathilde, who kept drying her eyes with her handkerchief as she went along.

Left to himself, M. Saval succeeded in putting everything around him in order. Then he lighted the wax-candles, and waited.

He waited for a quarter of an hour, half an hour, an hour. Romantin did not return. Then, suddenly there was a dreadful noise on the stairs, a song shouted out in chorus by twenty mouths and a regular march like that of a Prussian regiment. The whole house was shaken by the steady tramp of feet. The door flew open, and a motley throng appeared—men and women in file, two and two holding each other by the arm and stamping their heels on the ground to mark time, advanced into the studio like a snake uncoiling itself. They howled:

"Come, and let us all be merry,
Pretty maids and soldiers gay!"

M. Saval, thunderstruck, remained standing in evening dress under the chandelier. The procession of revellers caught sight of him, and uttered a shout:

"A Jeames! A Jeames!"

And they began whirling round him, surrounding him with a circle of vociferations. Then they took each other by the hand and went dancing about madly.

He attempted to explain:

"Messieurs—messieurs—mesdames——"

But they did not listen to him. They whirled about, they jumped, they brawled.

At last, the dancing ceased. M. Saval said:

"Gentlemen——"

A tall young fellow, fair-haired and bearded to the nose, interrupted him:

"What's your name, my friend?"

The notary, quite scared, said:

"I am M. Saval."

A voice exclaimed:

"You mean Baptiste."

A woman said:

"Let the poor waiter alone! You'll end by making him get angry.

He's paid to wait on us, and not to be laughed at by us."

Then, M. Saval noticed that each guest had brought his own provisions. One held a bottle of wine, and the other a pie. This one had a loaf of bread, and one a ham.

The tall, fair young fellow placed in his hands an enormous sausage, and gave orders:

"Here, go and arrange the sideboard in the corner over there. Put the bottles at the left and the provisions at the right."

Saval, getting quite distracted, exclaimed: "But, messieurs, I am a notary!"

There was a moment's silence and then a wild outburst of laughter. One suspicious gentleman asked:

"How came you to be here?"

He explained, telling about his project of going to the opera, his departure from Vernon, his arrival in Paris, and the way in which he had spent the evening.

They sat around him to listen to him; they greeted him with words of applause, and called him Scheherazade.

Romantin did not return. Other guests arrived. M. Saval was presented to them so that he might begin his story over again. He declined; they forced him to relate it. They seated and tied him on one of three chairs between two women who kept constantly filling his glass. He drank; he laughed; he talked; he sang, too. He tried to waltz with his chair, and fell on the ground.

From that moment, he forgot everything. It seemed to him, however, that they undressed him, put him to bed, and that he was nauseated.

When he awoke, it was broad daylight, and he lay stretched with his feet against a cupboard, in a strange bed.

An old woman with a broom in her hand was glaring angrily at him. At last, she said:

"Clear out, you blackguard! Clear out! What right has anyone to get drunk like this?"

He sat up in bed, feeling very ill at ease. He asked:

"Where am I?"

"Where are you, you dirty scamp? You are drunk. Take your rotten carcass out of here as quick as you can—and lose no time about it!"

He wanted to get up. He found that he was in no condition to do so. His clothes had disappeared. He blurted out:

"Madame, I——Then he remembered. What was he to do? He asked:

"Did Monsieur Romantin come back?"

The doorkeeper shouted:

"Will you take your dirty carcass out of this, so that he at any rate may not catch you here?"

M. Saval said, in a state of confusion:

"I haven't got my clothes; they have been taken away from me."

He had to wait, to explain his situation, give notice to his friends, and borrow some money to buy clothes. He did not leave Paris till evening. And when people talk about music to him in his beautiful drawing-room in Vernon, he declares with an air of authority that painting is a very inferior art.